"You have no one to trust."

Amber didn't need him reminding her.

"Well, now you've got me."

She turned a fierce gaze on him. "You are going to leave and forget you ever saw the boy or me."

Lance stood his ground. "That's not happening. You're stuck with me."

"I don't think you understand. The last two people who got involved with me are dead. I can't let that happen to you."

"And yet you came home," he said softly.

Only to get something she desperately needed.

She gave a humorless laugh. "Is there supposed to be some psychological meaning to that?"

"What do you think?"

She glanced toward the house. "Maybe there is. I've been in a lot of tight spots, but this time I might be in over my head."

"Then let me help."

She met his gaze. "You could be putting yourself in the kind of danger that people don't live to talk about."

He didn't flinch. "It wouldn't be the first time."

Lynette Eason is a bestselling, award-winning author who makes her home in South Carolina with her husband and two teenage children. She enjoys traveling, spending time with her family and teaching at various writing conferences around the country. She is a member of RWA (Romance Writers of America) and ACFW (American Christian Fiction Writers). Lynette can often be found online interacting with her readers. You can find her at Facebook.com/lynette.eason and on Twitter, @lynetteeason.

Books by Lynette Eason

Love Inspired Suspense

Wrangler's Corner

The Lawman Returns
Rodeo Rescuer
Protecting Her Daughter
Classified Christmas Mission

Rookie K-9 Unit

Honor and Defend

Capitol K-9 Unit

Trail of Evidence

Family Reunions

Hide and Seek
Christmas Cover-Up
Her Stolen Past

Rose Mountain Refuge

Agent Undercover
Holiday Hideout
Danger on the Mountain

Visit the Author Profile page at Harlequin.com for more titles.

CLASSIFIED CHRISTMAS MISSION

LYNETTE EASON

HARLEQUIN® LOVE INSPIRED® SUSPENSE

Recycling programs
for this product may
not exist in your area.

 LOVE INSPIRED BOOKS

ISBN-13: 978-0-373-44783-1

Classified Christmas Mission

Copyright © 2016 by Lynette Eason

www.Harlequin.com

Printed in U.S.A.

He will cover you with His feathers,
and under His wings you will find refuge;
His faithfulness will be your shield and rampart.
—*Psalms* 91:4

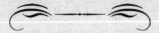

Dedicated to my family. I love you so much.

ONE

CIA officer Amber Starke pressed the gas pedal and prayed that she wouldn't slide over the cliff and into the ravine below. She was trying to escape killers, not plunge to her death because she got careless in bad weather. But she couldn't see the road she needed. It was around here somewhere, but her childhood memory was vague, the exact location of the drive refusing to rise to the surface. Of course it was dark and her windshield resembled a field of white.

The sun continued to drop along with the temperature and the snow-stressed windshield wipers slowed as ice started to form on them. Amber knew it would be time to find a place to hole up and she had just the destination in mind.

If they could get there.

She'd been driving for the last seventeen hours stopping only for restroom breaks and food. She hadn't planned to do so, but her young passenger hadn't protested so she'd kept going. Yesterday it had been fifteen hours of the same. She didn't know why Sam had been so agreeable in riding almost nonstop, but she just counted her blessings and kept going.

She glanced in the rearview mirror and breathed a sigh of relief at the sight of the sleeping child. The six-year-old who didn't like change had just had his life turned upside down. With a dead mother and killer for a father, Amber knew she was the child's only hope to live to see seven. She just prayed she could make that happen. But in order to do that, she had to figure out how to coax the secrets from his brain before his father caught up with them. Fortunately, Sam loved road trips. She had a feeling it was because there were very few distractions and plenty of game time on his phone to entertain him. She'd gotten him a special phone that was encrypted and untraceable. He didn't know that, but it sure made her feel better.

Amber saw the sharp curve ahead and lightly pressed the brakes. The sedan slowed, but she could feel the ice building on the road.

Great. She remembered the harsh winters from her childhood and this looked to be one of the harshest. She wanted to kick herself for not checking the weather before heading east from California, but getting away from the people trying to kill them had taken precedence.

The wipers continued to slow, becoming heavy with snow and she knew she couldn't keep going much longer. She had to get to the cabin. They'd be safe there, she was certain of it. In all the years she'd been with the agency she'd never been traced to her hometown of Wrangler's Corner. But the deciding factor in making a beeline for home was that she had documents, passports and money hidden away that would allow her and Sam to disappear for good. She just had to get to it.

She slapped the wheel. The weather! She did not

need this snow. Her brain kicked in, trying to come up with a plan should she need it.

She supposed as long as she could keep the car running and the heater on, they'd be all right but after a glance at the gas gauge, Amber saw that wasn't going to be an option. She was pushing empty. She hadn't liked the looks of the two men at the last gas station so had simply circled the pumps and kept going.

She might have enough to get to the cabin. She glanced behind her. Had she been followed? She didn't think so, but the people after her and Sam were good. Scary good. Her fingers flexed on the wheel. Her heart still cried for her friend, Sam's mother, who'd died two days ago, killed by Sam's father before the cancer could claim her life. She'd died too soon. A violent senseless death that caused the rage to boil in Amber's soul when the memories pressed in.

"Home. Number One Mom."

"What?" She looked in the rearview mirror. Sam was awake.

His dark eyes wouldn't meet hers. "Home." He clasped his arms around his middle and began his familiar rocking back and forth. "Go home."

She blinked against the tears that wanted to well. "Hey, Sam, I know you want to go home, but we can't right now, okay?"

"Home! Number One Mom."

With Sam's autism, Amber wasn't sure exactly what he understood and what he didn't. He was verbal sometimes. Other times the day would pass without him uttering a word. And he loved numbers. He numbered everything and it seemed to appease him even if she didn't have a clue what it was he was numbering. She knew Number One Mom referred to the woman who'd given him birth. Amber's friend who now lay cold in her grave.

One thing she'd learned while watching Sam grow up these past four years and becoming his Number Two Mom as he called her, no two autistic kids were alike so it was best to treat them individually. And Sam was definitely unique with a quirky personality and a photographic memory.

With her right hand, she reached into her purse that rested on the passenger seat and pulled out a different device. It held only one game and it was his favorite. She'd been saving it for just this moment. She held it toward him. "Here. You want to play?"

"Yes. Favorite game Number one game." He snatched it and powered it on.

"What do you say?"

"Thanks."

"You're welcome."

His head bent over the game, she breathed a sigh of relief. She'd known Sam since he was two. His mother, Nadia Pirhadi, had become her best friend after Amber had recruited her as an asset for the agency approximately four years ago. The woman had proven extremely capable. Forced into an arranged marriage by her family, she loathed her husband's evil activities and, unbeknownst to him, had vowed to use her position to bring him down. It had taken her almost six years to seize the opportunity to contact the CIA, but she'd managed to do it—and that brought Amber into her life. A deadly mistake as far as Amber was now concerned.

Her jaw tightened as she slowly rounded the curve. She should have known better. She'd been undercover so long, she'd relaxed her guard. Gotten slack. Whatever. She stiffened and looked back to check on Sam. His attention was ensnared by the game and her mind went back to Nadia.

No, she hadn't gotten slack. She'd been on edge for four years, though. She'd missed something. Something that should have told her Nadia's husband was suspicious, that he suspected his wife was snooping, looking for information to pass on to the CIA. But Amber had missed it and as a result, she'd gotten her best friend killed.

Now it was up to her to protect the woman's son and bring her killers to justice. Amber's jaw tightened. Being on US soil would serve in her best interests. If this had happened two weeks ago while she'd been in Ibirizstan, she'd really be in trouble. But Nadia had insisted that Amber accompany her to the States. She wanted her friend there to be her support while she saw the oncologist. And Amber hadn't been able to refuse. Nor had she wanted to.

She glanced in her rearview mirror and tightened her grip on the wheel. Headlights were coming up fast even on this growing-more-treacherous-by-the-minute back road. She ordered her pulse to slow. It could be nothing. Just someone who hadn't expected the weather to get so bad. She looked at Sam once more. He hadn't moved, his attention completely on the game in his hands.

She pressed the brake and the car slowed without a problem. The vehicle behind her slowed as well, the headlights still beaming in her back window. With her right hand, Amber lifted the edge of her sweatshirt and unclipped the strap that held her Glock 17 in the holster. She'd never carried a gun before the past week, but recent circumstances had dictated that she put her concealed weapons permit to use.

Another glance in the rearview mirror had her nerves tightening. The headlights were still there and closing in fast. She had a feeling that meant danger had found them. She curled her fingers around the weapon and pulled it from the holster.

Deputy Lance Goode figured he'd be at the Starke ranch in time to eat a home-cooked meal and catch the football game with brothers, Clay and Seth Starke. The Titans versus the Raiders. Should be a shutout, might even be a little boring, but he wanted to see it. Actually boring sounded good to him right now.

He'd made two arrests today. One for a DUI and the other for assault. Mark Jessup had broken his wife's nose, and she'd pressed charges. For now. He grimaced. Domestic violence. Not usually a problem in the small town of Wrangler's Corner, Tennessee, but this had been his third call to the home in the past three weeks and, as he suspected, the situation had escalated and the husband had finally done some real damage to his wife. So now the man could sit in a jail cell for a bit. At least until she dropped the charges. Which he knew she would.

In the meantime he planned to hang out with the Starkes. Lance knew they considered him a part of the family and, when he wasn't on duty, Sunday nights were the highlight of his week. He'd just punched himself off the clock, showered and changed clothes at the station. The only thing remaining from his uniform was the Glock 17 strapped to his hip. Now he was ready for some good food and fun.

Fighting to see through the drifting snow, Lance kept

the SUV steady, grateful for the chains on the tires. The forecast had called for cold and snow and the meteorologists had actually gotten it right for once. He wished they'd been wrong. His phone rang and he hit the button that would allow the call to come in through the speakers of his car. "Hello?"

"You headed over here?" Clay Starke asked.

"Should be there in about fifteen minutes."

"It's looking nasty out there. You have a bag in your car in case you need to stay the night?"

"Yep." He often stayed in the guest room on Sunday nights. Not because he didn't have anywhere else to stay, but because he was invited.

He caught sight of headlights just ahead on the sharp curve and slowed. "Let me go. I need to concentrate in this weather. You're right, it's getting nasty."

"Supposed to get nastier. See you in a few."

He hung up and focused on keeping the Ford Police Interceptor on his side of the road. The headlights came closer. Followed by a second set. Who was crazy enough to be out in this mess besides him?

He passed the first car and blinked. Even through the falling snow, he'd caught a glimpse of the driver when the wiper scraped the moisture from the windshield. Amber Starke? What was she doing here? Neither Clay nor Seth—and more importantly, Amber's mother—had mentioned she'd planned to come home for a visit. Or had they just neglected to mention it to him?

A loud crack split the quiet mountainside and Lance flinched then stepped on the brakes. His Interceptor responded beautifully in spite of the ice and he pulled to a stop. Chills swept over him. He'd heard that sound before. Had heard it often out here in the Tennessee hills. A gunshot.

When he looked back he saw Amber's SUV spin and then plunge over the side of the mountain. The vehicle behind her never stopped, just roared past.

For the third time that day, his adrenaline pumped into overdrive. He grabbed the radio just below the dash and called it in even as he executed a three-point turn in the middle of the freezing road.

"Lance?" Gretchen, the Wrangler's Corner second shift dispatcher, answered.

"I've got a wreck on Jasper Road, Gretch. I need some backup. And probably an ambulance."

"It's going to take them a while to get there in this mess."

"I know. I've got my first aid kit in the car. I'll be doing what I can. Just tell them to hurry." Trained as a first responder, he had the knowledge and the equipment to help. He just hoped it would be enough.

Gretchen put out the call and Lance pulled to a stop on the side of the road. His heart pounded as he climbed out, alert and looking to make sure the shooter wasn't doubling back.

He didn't see any sign of that so he headed to the edge to look over. He saw the tracks disappear under an overhang. He dropped to his knees and tried to see. Relief shot through him. Amber's SUV had only gone down the slight slope, under the overhang, and wedged itself between two trees. He could see the back of it, just barely jutting out. Now he just had to find out if the bullet had done any bodily damage.

He looked at the space between him and her car. White space. It looked like snow, but could be ice. He ran to the back of his SUV and opened the back. He grabbed the hundred-foot-length rope that he always carried with him and hefted it over his shoulder with a grunt. He lugged it to the front of the Ford and tied one end to the grill then tossed the rest down to Amber's car. It reached, but barely. It would have to do. With one more glance over his shoulder, he grasped hold of the rope and slipped and slid down the embankment to the car. Once he reached the back, he was able to duck under the overhang and squeeze himself between the rock and the driver's door.

Amber lay against the wheel, eyes closed. Fear shot through. *Please let her be all right.* He reached for the door handle and pulled it open. It hit the rock, but there was enough room for her to get out if she wasn't too badly hurt.

Amber lifted her head, and he found himself staring down the barrel of a gun.

TWO

Amber processed who stood before her and lowered her weapon with relief. "Lance?"

"Yeah. Are you all right? Someone shot at you!"

She scowled. "I'm fine." She hadn't been hurt when she'd placed her head on the steering wheel, she just wanted the person who approached the car to think she was. "And I sort of figured out that someone was shooting, thanks." Sam! She released her seat belt and spun to see the boy staring at them, the game still clutched in his hand. He was safe. Unhurt, as well. His seat belt had done the job. His gaze flicked from her to Lance then back to her. Then down to the game he still clutched. He wasn't even fazed—or curious about what had just happened.

"I've got backup on the way," Lance said. "Let's get you two out of the car and into mine. I've got the heater running."

She snapped her head up. "Cancel that backup. We're fine and don't need help."

"What?"

She hated repeating herself. Especially when she was in a hurry. "Tell them we're fine and they don't need to come."

"I can't do that. Someone *shot* at you. There will be an investigation."

She shoved out of the vehicle. "There can't be an investigation because no one can know I'm here, you understand? This never happened." He gaped, then narrowed his eyes and tightened his jaw. She ran a shaky hand through her hair. Great. Now what? This was Lance, the most stubborn man in the town. She was going to have to read him in. But first—"Help me get Sam to the old Landers cabin and I'll explain everything."

"That cabin's been empty since June. After Mrs. Landers died, her kids didn't want anything to do with it."

"I know. That's the point." She popped the trunk and pulled the two backpacks from it. She'd have to get the suitcase later.

"You can't leave the scene of the accident."

"I don't have a choice. No one else is involved, no one is hurt. I can leave. Now you can be a friend and help me or stay here, but we're leaving. And don't tell anyone you saw me or Sam, got it?"

"Why?"

She wanted to stomp her foot and yell at him. Instead she took a deep breath. "Because whoever just shot at us and ran us off the road isn't going to stop there. They'll be back, and I want to be gone when they show back up."

"Why is someone trying to kill you?"

Frustration pounded through her. "I don't have time to explain right now. Help me get to the cabin and I'll tell you everything."

He hesitated for a fraction of a second more then gave a low groan and punched his phone's screen with quick jabs. "Gretchen? Yeah. Cancel the backup. Yes, I'm sure. We're good."

Lance grabbed the backpacks from her. Amber moved to the back passenger door on the side away from the overhang, reached in and grabbed two heavy coats from where they'd fallen to the floorboard. "Come on, Sam, we have to go." He ignored her. The sirens grew closer then went silent. "Sam. Number One Mom would want you to come with me."

He didn't look up, but scooted across the seat and out the door, his gaze still on his game. She gave a sigh of relief. She never was very sure what would work with him and what wouldn't. Telling him his mother wanted him to do something seemed wrong, but if it was to save his life she'd do it. She held his coat for him and after a brief hesitation, he allowed her to help him put it on. She zipped it and pulled a hat on his head. "Gloves are in your pockets, Sam." He simply stood there. "Sam? Your hands will get cold if you don't put on the gloves." She reached for the first pocket and he stepped back.

"No."

She placed a hand on his arm and he didn't pull away. She was never sure if she could touch him or not. They'd forgo the gloves for now. "Sam, I have to hold you while we walk up with the rope, okay?"

"Will he let me piggyback him?" Lance asked.

"No. Probably not." She slipped her arms into her coat and zipped it. Then she got Sam's attention and pointed. "See? We have to climb the rope up to the top." He didn't acknowledge her. She wrapped an arm around his waist with one hand and grasped the rope with the other. "Walk with me, Sam." At first he resisted. Tried to pull away from her. She let him go and he slipped and fell on his rear. She held out a hand. "I have to help you, okay?" She reached for his arm again and helped him up. When he didn't pull away, she scooted him behind her. "Walk in my steps. Count how many steps it takes to get to the top, will you?" She started off again, Lance staying silent behind Sam. She knew if the boy fell again, he'd catch him.

This time Sam put one foot in front of the other. "Good job, Sam." He was either too distracted to notice her touch or just didn't care at the moment. He let her lead, stepping carefully into the footprints she left in the snow. He held the game at his side, forgotten in this new adventure of "step in Amber's steps." His other hand clutched her belt and she heard him counting under his breath.

Amber led the way, memories of exploring these woods with her brothers and Lance crowded her mind. She'd had a great childhood, running free without a care in the world—except when one of those brothers took it upon himself to tease her…or scare her…or talk her into doing something that would get her in trouble with her parents. Yes, those were good times. Times that seemed like a hundred years ago.

And now she was running from killers. With a special-needs child to keep safe. She'd do it or die trying, but she had to admit, the responsibility scared her to death. Almost more than being caught by the people chasing them. Once they were in Lance's car, she would find the road that led to the cabin. Or she could just let Lance get them there.

She glanced at the man beside her. He would remember which road to take.

She kept her gun within reach, nerves humming since she halfway expected someone to jump out of the trees. But that was silly. Finally, she crested the hill. She let go of the rope and led Sam to stand next to the Ford.

"Why is someone shooting at you?" Lance said as he caught up with her.

He wanted to discuss this now? "Because I have something they want."

She spotted the road she'd been looking for. "And there it is. We almost made it." The exertion had kept them warm but she knew that once they weren't moving, she would be cold. Very cold. "How many steps, Sam?"

"Sixty-seven."

He always answered her questions about numbers. Such an interesting kid. And she loved him fiercely.

"The cabin's not too far from here," Lance said. "Get in and I'll take you there."

She opened the back door for Sam then paused. "No, wait." She shut the door. "You can't take us, we need to walk through the woods."

"Are you crazy?"

"Getting that way. If the people who shot at me come back, they'll see the tracks and know I went off the road. Then they'll look for tracks leading away. If you drive us, you'll leave fresh tracks straight from here to the cabin."

"What about your footprints?"

She looked up. It was snowing fast enough to fill shallow steps but not the deep grooves his SUV would make. Maybe. "I'll just have to take that chance. As long as we're moving through the woods, we should be all right."

"What if you walk along the edge of the lake?"

"And let the water cover our tracks?"

"And come up to the house from the back. They'll be looking for tracks on this side."

She looked at Sam.

He tilted his head and looked at the ground. "Hungry. Number five for six forty-nine plus add cheese for ninety-nine cents and a number twenty-four for two ninety-nine. The subtotal is ten forty-seven plus sixty-three cents for tax. The grand total is eleven dollars and ten cents."

Lance lifted a brow. "A human calculator?"

"Something like that. And he likes lists."

"I guess we know what he wants for dinner," Lance said. "What restaurant?"

"Burgers-N-Shakes To Go. But that's going to have to wait."

She picked up the pace and looked back to make sure Sam was still in her footsteps. He was. And Lance was right behind Sam.

She heard the car on the road behind them before she saw it. She spun and motioned for Lance to get behind a tree. But he was already moving, crossing the street to the wooded area. He stashed the backpacks and drew his weapon then slid behind the large oak and faced the road.

Amber did the same. "Sam, over here. Hurry." Sam didn't look up, just trudged toward her. She positioned him where she wanted him. He was small enough that she knew he was invisible from the road. "Stay here, okay? Don't move. Count how many seconds we stand here quiet without making a sound. Start now."

He didn't look at her but he didn't move either. She just prayed that he stayed that way. She took cover behind one of the other larger trees nearest to Sam. If she had to grab him and run, she would. The car slowed, looking at the SUV parked on the edge of the road. She knew her car wasn't visible from where the sedan was positioned, but if they got out and looked close, it would be. She held her breath and caught Lance's eye. He was ready to act should he need to.

The car was the same one she'd seen behind her just a while ago. The same one the bullet had come from. The same one that had been parked in Yousef Pirhadi's driveway the morning she'd run with Sam. How had they found her?

Lance didn't know the whole story, but he knew he had to help Amber and Sam. The car next to his SUV sat still and idled. He wondered if the occupants were talking about whether they should explore the area. If they got out and started looking around, Lance figured they'd be discovered.

A fire truck lumbered into view and Lance nearly went to his knees with gratitude. It moved slowly, carefully plowing its way through the few inches of snow that hadn't yet frozen.

The sedan gently pulled away from the scene appearing not to be in a hurry. Anyone watching would just assume he'd slowed to check on the accident victims but decided to leave when help arrived. Lance released a breath and saw Amber do the same. She shoved her weapon out of sight and touched Sam on the arm. Sam ignored her. "Come on, Sam, time to go."

Again, the boy didn't move and Amber sighed.

Lance spotted the video game sitting on the ground. "He might need this." Lance picked it up and handed it to Sam.

Sam took it. "Thanks."

"You're welcome."

Lance picked up the backpacks and passed them to her. "I've got to address this. I guess they decided to check the scene in spite of my canceling the call. Head to the cabin. I'll be there shortly."

"You won't mention us?"

He sighed. "No, I won't mention you. But we're going to have a long talk when I get there."

She nodded. "Fine. Thank you. And if you can avoid having them find the car just yet, I would appreciate it."

He drew in a breath. "All right. I'll do my best."

"I just need to buy some time. I know someone will see the car sooner or later, I just need later, okay?"

"Like I said, I'll try. Watch out for that sedan. Keep the same plan. Stay in these woods and cross the street before you get to the house. Cut through the beachy area of the lake and come up to the back of the house. There should be a key under the turtle in the flower bed."

"That's what I was counting on." She touched Sam's hand and he let her begin to lead him out of the woods and, hopefully, toward safety.

Lance watched them until they disappeared over the next rise then down the hill. Then he turned and made his way back across the street to answer the questions as best he could. He pulled his phone from the clip on his belt and saw he had six missed calls. All from Clay,

Amber's brother. He pressed the button to dial the man's number and lifted the phone to his ear. Clay answered on the first ring. "Are you all right?"

"Yes. I came across an accident and stopped to help." All truth. He wouldn't lie to his boss.

"You need me to come out there?" Clay obviously hadn't heard about the wreck—or the fact that Lance had called for backup and then canceled it. Hopefully, by the time that was revealed, Amber would have agreed to bring her brother in on whatever was going on with her.

"No, but I'm going to be a while. Fortunately, there aren't any injuries or fatalities, but you know how it goes. This is going to take some time."

"Right. How's the weather holding for you?"

Lance looked at the sky and the white ground around him. "The snow's stopped falling but the temperature hasn't. It's going to be a cold one."

"Stay warm."

"Yeah, you, too."

"Want me to save you a plate?"

Lance thought about it. He wasn't going to leave Amber and Sam at the cabin alone. She needed someone to watch her back and he knew that she wasn't going to ask for help. He felt guilty, torn between letting Clay know his sister needed help and keeping her secret like she'd asked. He'd keep his word, but he didn't like it—or think it was right. However, if he spilled the story to Clay and it put Amber and Sam in even more danger...

Lance sighed. "No. I may not make it tonight after all. If you don't see me, don't worry about it. I'll check in with you later."

"If you're sure."

Lance glanced in the direction Amber and Sam had gone. "I'm sure." Maybe by the time he heard Amber's story and put the pieces to this puzzle together, he'd think of a way to convince her to bring her brother, the sheriff of Wrangler's Corner, into her small circle of trust.

THREE

Amber put one wet, frozen foot in front of the other as she led the way to the cabin. Her adrenaline was crashing and so was her energy. She'd been awake almost two straight days. If she didn't get some sleep soon, her body was going to quit on her. Fortunately, Sam was in a good mood and seemed content to follow her lead. Of course, he'd slept a good bit of the drive and she'd just carried him through the water so his feet would stay dry. Once she explained to him why she needed to carry him, he acquiesced. Sometimes logic worked with him, sometimes not. She was thankful he'd made it easy on her this time.

Amber finally reached the flower bed and pulled her gloves from her hands. She dug through the dirt and leaves in the place she knew the turtle used to be. Her fingers touched a hard surface, and she brushed the refuse away. It was still there. "Thank you, God. Now please, let the key be there, too," she whispered.

"Thank you, God," Sam mimicked her.

Amber lifted the turtle and the once-silver key lay on the small patch of dirt. She snatched it up and headed for the back door. Sam plodded along beside her. She shivered. "You ready to get warmed up?"

He didn't answer and she didn't expect him to. She tested the knob and it was locked as she'd figured it would be. She inserted the key and twisted. Nothing. What? "Oh come on," she muttered. She tried again. Still nothing. She slapped the door with her palm. Tried the key again.

And it turned.

She sucked in a breath and pushed the door open. "Hello? Anyone here?" She didn't think so, but it didn't hurt to use a bit of caution. She kept her hand on her weapon and Sam behind her. "Hello?" The house echoed back at her. The musty odor filled her nose, and she knew no one had been in the home for a while. It was cold inside. Almost as cold as it was outside.

She just prayed the power and water were still on. Her stomach rumbled reminding her they needed to eat something. The beef jerky, jar of peanut butter and bag of crackers in the backpack might have to suffice.

She pushed the door open farther and stepped inside. Her feet felt like blocks of ice but she couldn't do anything about that just yet. Sam followed and she shut and locked the door behind him. "All right, let's see if this works." She reached for the light switch and flipped it up. A low glow came from the lamp on the end table. She let out a small breath of relief. Power was on. Now to clear the house. She checked on Sam who huddled in his coat, his game still clutched in his right hand. "You okay?"

"Yes." Sam walked to the couch and sat down. Amber blinked at the fact that he'd answered her this time. She'd never figure out how his mind worked. And that was okay. For the past four years that she'd known Sam, she'd followed Nadia's example and talked to him like she would any other six-year-old. Sometimes he answered, sometimes he didn't.

She leaned over and unlaced her wet boots and kicked them off. Her socks squished against the hardwoods as she made her way to the thermostat on the wall. If the power was on, there should be heat, right? *Please let there be heat, God.*

Because she really didn't feel like trying to find dry wood to start a fire in the fireplace.

She flipped the switch and heard a rumble in the back of the house as the furnace came to life. *Oh, thank You, thank You.* The Landerses' children might not have wanted anything to do with the cabin, but they'd been paying the power bill. Which meant they probably had water, too. She searched the cabin for a laundry room and found the stackable washer and dryer in the hall. Just where she remembered it being.

Amber pulled her socks off, grabbed her boots and threw them in the dryer. It started right up, but the *thunk, thunk* of her boots had her worried. She found several towels in the bathroom and tossed them in with her boots. Now the *thunks* were muted, and she didn't think anyone would be able to hear it from outside. She turned the oven on high and opened the door. It would heat fast and help warm the area. She'd be sure to turn it down as soon as they were comfortable.

She could smell the odor from the heating unit. It hadn't been used in a while. At the sink, she turned on the faucet and water rushed into the basin and swirled down the drain.

Perfect.

She turned to see Sam still in his coat, sitting on the sofa and playing his game. Amber walked over to him and unlaced his boots. "Might as well get comfortable, kiddo." She sighed and looked at the shoes in her hands. The sole of the left one was coming off. "We're going to have to get you some new shoes soon."

"No new shoes. Boots."

"Okay. New boots then."

"No. Old boots." He fell silent and continued to focus on the game.

Amber pursed her lips. "What is it about these boots that you like so much anyway?"

Sam didn't acknowledge her question and she didn't force the issue. He had two pairs of shoes he'd wear without a tantrum. The ones she'd just removed from his feet and the pair sitting in his closet at the home he'd never return to.

She set the boots on the floor, walked to the windows near the back door and glanced out. Darkness had fallen but the full moon allowed her to see fairly well outside. The lake looked like a dark pool of black ink surrounded by trees and white snow. She could see her footsteps leading up from the lake and prayed that the people after them wouldn't think to look in the backyards of the homes surrounding the lake. Or that the once-again falling snow would fill in the tracks before they started looking.

Amber moved to the front windows, scanning the area. The driveway branched off into a side road that led to the main road she'd been traveling when the goons had shot at her.

She glanced at her phone. Her untraceable throwaway phone. And was very tempted to dial her brother Clay's number. She bit her lip, indecision warring inside her. Her handler would be waiting for her to call, to let her know where she was. Or did she already know?

For the first time since her flight with Sam, she had a moment to think. Kathryn Petrov. Her handler and friend, a woman Amber could trust with her life. Or so she thought. She and Kat had been through a lot together, and she never would have imagined the woman capable of betrayal. Now she didn't know what to think or who to trust.

The knock on the door froze her for a split second. Sam didn't bother to look up from his game. Amber slid her weapon into her hand and stepped on bare feet over to the door.

Another knock. "Amber, it's me, Lance. Let me in. I'm freezing."

She slid her gun back into the holster and opened the door. When he stepped inside, he squished. "You walked in the lake, too?" she asked.

"Yes. I walked in your prints. I left my SUV at the site of the wreck." He held up a suitcase. "But I brought this."

"Oh, thank you." She took it from him. "Take your shoes and socks off, we'll throw them in the dryer."

While he discarded his wet boots and pulled his socks off, she opened the dryer and checked on hers. "Still a bit soggy. Might as well add yours to them."

Lance padded over in his bare feet and handed her the wet socks and shoes. She tossed them in the dryer and got it started once again and hoped they wouldn't have to leave the cabin in a hurry.

When she turned to face him, her nose collided with his chest and his hands came up to grip her elbows. She lifted her head, her heart thudding into overdrive. And there it was. The attraction she'd felt for him since…oh, forever. The childhood crush she'd never outgrown. She remembered the crushing despair when she'd learned that he'd married someone else. And as a result, she'd thrown herself into her job to push his memory aside. It had worked for a while. But now…now Krissy, his wife, was dead and he'd been alone for a long time. Had his heart healed from his wife's betrayal and criminal activities? Was he ready to find someone else? And why was she even wondering?

She swallowed and tried to figure out her next move. Close in for a kiss or step back and pretend she didn't see the spark of interest in his brown eyes?

He took the decision out of her hands. He cleared his throat. "So, do you have time to talk?"

Disappointed that the choice was suddenly gone, she tilted her head and kept her gaze on his. "Of course. Tell me what happened at the scene."

"I answered a lot of questions and managed to keep them from finding the car. For now. If you look over the edge, you can't see the vehicle immediately. When you hit those trees, snow fell and covered the top of it. There's also a small overhang that sort of hides it, so…" He shrugged. "I don't know. I'm not sure Gretchen was convinced everything was fine, but I did manage to buy the time you said you needed."

"Good," she breathed as relief filled her. "What about the tracks I left going down the side?"

"I parked my SUV over most of them to hide them."

"Thank you."

"Of course everyone wanted to know what happened to the person involved."

She winced. "What did you say?"

"That the person involved walked away from the wreck and was going to be fine. Although I did kind of hint at an abusive relationship and the longer we gave the person to get away the better off she'd be. They quit asking questions after that."

She blew out a low breath. "Well, it's the truth. Sort of. Thanks."

He nodded and rubbed his hands together. "It's starting to warm up in here."

"Finally." She walked over, shut the oven off and closed the door.

"I can't believe the power and water are still on."

"And no one's broken in," she added.

"That's due to the security that patrols this area. You're going to have to keep a low profile if you want to stay here very long."

"I don't plan to be here too long. I'm hoping to get what I need and get moving again."

"What you need?"

"Yes."

"Okay, I guess that brings us full circle. Who shot at you, Amber? Who are you running from and why?"

Amber pursed her lips then motioned for him to have a seat at the kitchen table. Instead, he walked to the window and looked out. He placed his wallet and keys on the end table next to the sofa. "It's quiet in the back."

"Yes. For now." She pushed aside the curtain above the sink. "The front is, too." She scanned the area. "No headlights, no shadows. The full moon is helpful."

"How did they find you?"

"I have my theories."

"Such as?"

"A tracker on my vehicle. One that I didn't find in spite of my careful search. Maybe."

"Ah."

Lance pulled out a chair and planted himself there. Amber turned and opened the freezer. "Oh, thank You, God," she breathed.

"What?"

"Food." She turned back to him with a frown. "Are you sure no one's been living here?"

He shrugged and rubbed his head. "Now that I think about it, Mrs. Landers's grandson may have been here sometime last month around Thanksgiving."

"Then all the food in this freezer is probably good."

"You're going to eat it?"

Her frown deepened. "I'll pay him for whatever I take, but yes, if it means the difference between going hungry and eating this food, we'll eat."

"Of course, I didn't mean you should starve."

She smiled. "I know. And I understand that I've just broken into someone else's home. Then again Mrs. Landers always liked me. She taught my Sunday school class when I was in middle school and she used to have us girls over to hang out and go waterskiing in the summertime. She was always telling me to make myself at home. I think she'd be more than happy to offer her help if she could."

He knew she was right, but still…the law was the law. Then again, someone had just tried to kill her and for now, this cabin was a safe place for her and Sam. Sam, who hadn't budged when Lance walked in. Sam, who wanted a hamburger and fries and a chocolate shake. Lance sighed. Their talk could wait until they'd eaten. He stood. "You have any hamburger meat in there?"

"Yep." She pulled out the patties and passed them to him.

At least the kid would have his burger. "Get me a frying pan. We'll see if they're still good."

"You cook?"

"Out of survival, but yes."

She dug in the cabinet next to the sink and came up with a frying pan. She handed it to him. "Have at it. I'm going to check on Sam then check all the windows again. I would walk outside, but don't want to leave any more footprints than we already have."

He frowned, but nodded. It was still hard to wrap his brain around the fact that Amber was here. She left and he turned the stove on. Within minutes Lance had the burgers cooking.

When he turned, he nearly ran Sam over. The boy stood behind him, watching him. "Hi."

"Hi."

"You like hamburgers, I hear."

"Hamburgers. Yes."

"Well, they'll be ready shortly. You know how to set the table?"

"Three plates, three forks, three glasses, three napkins."

"That should work."

"Three hamburgers, three pieces of cheese, three tomato slices, three squirts of ketchup, three squirts of mayonnaise, three buns."

"I hate it, but I don't think we have all that." Lance turned back to the stove and pressed the spatula against the meat. The smell made his stomach rumble, so he was going to go with the conclusion that the meat was fine to eat. He opened the pantry and found a bag of chips, a half-opened pack of cookies and a bag of dried fruit. He checked the dates. All good.

Now that he had time to think about it, he remembered overhearing someone at the diner in town talking about the fact that Jason Landers was going to sell the place. He glanced at the window. New curtains. He looked at the cabinets. They'd been repainted. Yep, Jason had been here working, fixing up the place. He hoped the man didn't show up anytime soon or they were going to have some explaining to do.

He opened the cabinet and pulled down three plates and three glasses. He handed them to Sam who put them on the table. Lance noticed the boy's precise movements. The plates went exactly in front of the chairs, the glasses just to the right of the plates.

Lance handed him the silverware from the drawer. Again, Sam placed them perfectly. "Nice job."

"Yes. Nice job. Hungry."

"We'll eat in just a couple of minutes. As soon as Amber gets back in here, all right?"

As though she'd heard him, she came from the back of the cabin and crossed the small den into the kitchen. "Wow, this looks great."

"Just burger patties tonight, I'm afraid. No buns or salad, but we've got chips and dried fruit."

She waved a hand. "Protein is good. All of that is perfect. I've got peanut butter and crackers if we need them."

"French fries," Sam said.

Amber bit her lip. "We don't have any fries tonight, Sam, I'm sorry. Eat the chips, though, they're made from potatoes just like French fries." She watched him carefully and Lance wondered if she was trying to guess how the boy would react.

She let out a breath when he simply sat and stared at his plate. Lance doled out the three burgers and the rest of the food and they ate them in silence.

Sam finished his last bite. "Television, please."

Amber looked up. "There's one in the bedroom. Come with me and we'll get you set up." She shot a look back over her shoulder at Lance and he interpreted it to mean they'd talk when she had Sam distracted.

He cleaned up the kitchen, leaving it cleaner than he'd found it, then walked into the den to check the windows once again. As he stared out into the night his gut twisted. What was Amber involved in? Who was after her and Sam? And why did he have a feeling his life was going to get flipped upside down?

Amber walked back into the living area and moved from window to window, doing exactly what he'd done just moments before. "CIA?" he asked.

She turned to face him, her face blank. "What?"

"You're with the CIA, aren't you?"

"Why do you ask?"

"Just answer the question."

She hesitated and he could almost see her thinking about lying. Finally, she frowned. "Yes. What gave it away?"

Lance shrugged. "The fact that I know you. The fact that your family believes you're a travel writer and the articles that come out don't sound like anything you might write."

She raised her eyes at that statement and he shrugged.

"Yes, I read them. Then there's the fact that you've missed a lot of important family milestones and I don't think anything less than life or death would have kept you away from being here for those. A travel article wouldn't have kept you away. And also the fact that you handle yourself like a trained professional. It just fits. Now that I think about it anyway."

She pursed her lips and nodded. "I came home for Thanksgiving."

"Last year. And then you missed Christmas. And Aaron and Zoe's wedding this past June."

Her jaw tightened. "It couldn't be helped."

"I'm beginning to understand that. But what really kind of gave it away was that you found Zoe's brother, Toby, and brought him with you for Christmas, for Zoe." Aaron Starke had fallen in love with Zoe Collier, a woman who'd been trying to keep her nine-year-old daughter, Sophia, safe from people who'd been trying to kidnap her. Aaron and Zoe had fallen in love and been married almost six months ago. "Then the day after Christmas, you two disappeared together because you had work that wouldn't wait." She pressed her lips together. "So that brings me to my next question," he said.

"Which is?"

"Why haven't you contacted your handler?"

"How do you know I haven't?"

"Call it instinct."

"I was on assignment in Ibirizstan and only one person in the world knew where I was."

"Your handler."

"Yep."

"Is your cover blown?"

"Wide open."

"And you think he had something to do with that?"

She sighed and checked the windows again. "She.

And I don't know. Before that happened, I would have trusted her without thought. But now… I was in California three days ago. My informant was killed. Her name was Nadia Pirhadi. She was my best friend and Sam is her son. I've been living with her and her family for the past four years working as Sam's nanny." Her jaw worked as though holding back emotion and Lance found himself wanting to go to her, to hold her. He curled his fingers into fists and forced himself to remain still. "When everything went south, I grabbed my car keys, Sam and bolted."

"And everyone thinks you're a travel writer."

"That's what they're supposed to think."

He rubbed his eyes then looked at her. "So what makes you think your handler is involved?"

"Because as I was leaving, I heard Sam's father, who'd just killed Sam's mother, yell my name."

Realization hit him. "Your real name, not your covert name."

"Yes. He called me Amber."

"And now you have no one to trust and nowhere to turn."

"Exactly."

"Well now you've got me. And you need to read in Clay."

She twisted her fingers together then released them to rub her eyes. "I would rather not involve him."

"He can help us."

She turned a fierce gaze on him. "There is no *us*. You're going to leave and go back to your normal life and forget that you ever saw Sam or me."

Lance stared at her for a brief moment before letting out a humorless laugh. "Well, I can tell you right now, that's not happening. You're stuck with me for the duration."

"I don't think you understand. The last two people who've gotten involved with me have died. I can't let that happen to you or anyone else."

"And yet you came home," he said softly.

She paused. "What?"

"You ran home."

"Yes, but it's just a pop in, pop out kind of thing. I left something here that I needed."

"But you left it here. At home."

"Yes." She gave a short humorless laugh. "Is there supposed to be some deep psychological meaning to that?"

"I don't know. What do you think?"

She stood frozen for a millisecond then her jaw trembled. "Maybe there is," she whispered. She glanced toward the back of the house. "I've been in a lot of tight spots over the last five years, but this time, it's very possible I'm in over my head."

"Then let us help."

She paused. Paced from window to window then turned and met his gaze. "If you help me, you could be putting yourself in the kind of danger that a lot people don't live to talk about."

He didn't flinch. "It wouldn't be the first time."

FOUR

Once Amber had helped Sam get a quick sponge bath and into some clean sweats and a long-sleeved T-shirt, she waited for him to climb beneath the covers. But then he pushed the blankets away and sat up. "Book. Number One Mom read a book. Please."

"Number One Mom isn't here, Sam, I'm sorry."

He blinked. "Number One Mom is gone."

"Yes, she is, Sam. She…died." She didn't know how much he understood, but he seemed to grasp the concept that his mother wasn't coming back. Maybe. In some ways he was brilliant and yet, he was definitely still a six-year-old child.

"Number Two Mom read a book. Please."

Amber opened the app on his phone and brought up his favorite book. A book about dogs and numbers. She read it to him three times before she saw his eyes getting heavy. She closed the app and plugged the phone in next to him. She wasn't a huge fan of allowing children his age unlimited use of technology, but right now, in their situation, she had to use whatever she could to keep him happy. Once she knew they were safe and his father was either in prison or dead, then they would re-evaluate the device usage.

Amber walked back into the den to find Lance standing at the window, his weapon held by his side. She tensed. "What is it?"

"Thought I heard something, but then I caught sight of a doe so maybe I'm just twitchy."

"Being twitchy might just keep us alive."

"Right." After twenty minutes and nothing else happening, she was finally able to relax a fraction. "I'm going to look in on Sam."

He nodded. Amber walked down the hall to peer in on the child. He lay sprawled on his back, his chest rising and falling with each even breath. *Keep him safe, God, no matter how You feel about me, keep that child safe, please. He's so smart, brilliant really. I know You have some kind of special plan for him. Let him live to fulfill that.* She felt tears prick at the back of her eyes and swallowed. Crying accomplished nothing. She wouldn't start now. Amber returned to the den and found Lance at the back door, peering out the window. He glanced at her when she entered. "How's he doing?"

"Sleeping. I'm not too surprised. He slept some in the car. It seemed like he slept a lot, but now that I think about it was more like catnaps. He needs a good night's rest."

"As do you, probably."

She couldn't help the yawn that escaped. "Mmm. Probably." She walked to the dryer and checked her socks. Dry. Perfect. The boots were still damp so she left them in and started the dryer again. She handed Lance his socks and then sat in the nearest chair to pull hers on.

"Go get the rest, Amber."

Amber hesitated. She'd had to rely on herself for so long that trusting someone else—even Lance Goode—wasn't a likely possibility. "I probably wouldn't fall asleep anyway."

"You've got to or you're going to get punchy and careless. Trust me, I know."

Amber rubbed her gritty eyes. It had been all she could do to stay awake and read to Sam. She sighed. Lance was right, of course. She had to sleep. "All right. There's a couch in Sam's room. I'll go try."

"What about the other bedroom? That would be more comfortable."

"No, I want to stay close to Sam. If he wakes up in a strange place he might get scared and start to wander. I'll be fine." He frowned but didn't protest. "Wake me in a few hours and you can take a turn."

He nodded and she headed back down the hall to the room where Sam slept. Sam rolled over and opened his eyes when she walked in. She went to him and placed a hand on his shoulder. "Go back to sleep, Sam. It's all right."

His eyes closed, and she waited for him to drift off again. When she was convinced he was once again sleeping soundly, she snagged a pillow from the other side of the bed, a musty blanket from the closet and made herself as comfortable as possible on the couch. She didn't expect to sleep but told herself she could at least relax a little. Her lids closed and she breathed deep.

Lance rubbed his forehead and moved to another window. It had been three hours since Amber had disappeared into Sam's room, and Lance had just looked in on them. They were both asleep in spite of Amber's allegation she wouldn't be able to. He'd figured she would. Her fatigue had rolled off her in waves. He'd pulled the boots out of the dryer and put his on. He'd placed hers by the couch where she now rested. She'd opened her eyes briefly when he'd entered, saw what he was doing and shut them again.

He glanced from her to the sleeping child and shook his head. It was a huge responsibility that she was taking on and he had to admire her determination. He just prayed she let people help her before it was too late.

From his position by the window, Lance caught a glimpse of shadowy movement in the trees near the edge of the drive. He pulled his weapon and narrowed his eyes. Another deer? Or something more sinister? He waited and watched the area.

Nothing.

But he knew he'd seen something.

And then it moved again. Someone was behind the trees. Tension flooded him. His pulse picked up speed and his brain flashed scenarios. Then the shadow broke away and slipped to the next tree closer to the house. Lance saw the rifle in the figure's hands.

He snagged his phone from the clip on his belt, huffed a breath of relief that he had a signal and dialed his dispatcher even as he moved down the hall to wake Amber. "Gretchen, I need that backup after all. Send it to the Landers cabin. And now."

"What's going on, Lance? You need backup then you don't. Now you do."

"I'll explain later. Just get me the backup." He hung up. At the bedroom door, he paused. "Amber," he whispered.

Her eyes opened immediately and she sat up. Whatever she saw in his face had her reaching for the weapon that hadn't left her side. In one smooth move she swung her feet over the side of the couch. She found the boots, slipped her feet in and fastened the Velcro straps. She stood, weapon palmed and ready. She nodded and Lance led the way back into the den area. "What is it?" she asked as soon as they were in the hall with the door cracked.

"Someone's outside," Lance said. "I saw his rifle."

"They found the footprints."

"That's my guess."

She took the front window while he watched the back. Fortunately, the room was small enough that they could communicate without yelling.

"See anything out the front?" he asked, keeping his voice low.

"No, what about you?"

"Not at the moment. How many are there?"

"Probably two." She checked her weapon again. "The good thing is, they probably don't expect you to be here."

"I walked in your footsteps so..."

"Exactly. So it just looks like me alone, although they probably figured I'd carry Sam."

The glass shattered in front of his face and he jerked back, left cheek stinging. Cold air rushed in, and he lifted his weapon to fire back two quick rounds. The front window ruptured.

"Sam!" Amber fired three shots in the direction the bullets had come from then raced down the hallway to the bedroom.

Silence fell for a moment, and Lance figured their attackers were assessing the situation. They hadn't expected someone to fire back from both sides of the house. Amber reappeared with Sam in her arms, the child wrapped in the comforter from the bed. She stayed in the windowless hallway and set Sam on the floor. "Stay here, Sam, understand?" The child looked sleepy and a little grumpy, but otherwise unalarmed. Amber handed him the ever-present game but he simply set it on the floor beside him, laid down and closed his eyes.

Amber flinched when the gunfire started up again. More bullets riddled the walls of the cabin and shattered the windows in the kitchen. She swung her weapon to aim through the broken window in the den and fired back. "We've got to get out of here," she gasped. More bullets came her way, and she jerked back against the end table next to the sofa. The lamp crashed to the floor, and she didn't have time to worry about it. She caught sight of movement to the left, aimed and squeezed the trigger once more. The figure cried out, stumbled and went to his knees.

"Help should be on the way," Lance said. "I called dispatch. I'm not even sure they'll be able to get here, but I'm hoping if they do, the sirens will send these goons running."

"I think I hit one," she said. She fell silent as she studied the front area and waited for the sound of gunshots to ring through the night air once again. When it didn't, she looked back at Sam. He lay still where she'd put him, his eyes watchful, trusting.

He sat up. "One thirteen."

Amber blinked. "What?"

"One thirteen."

"One hundred thirteen? What does that mean, Sam?"

"Paper said one thirteen." Then he laid his head back on the floor and closed his eyes.

Amber knew Sam had just told her something very important, but she had no clue what it meant. And she didn't have time to think about it now. She had to get them out of the cabin and to a safe place.

She heard the roar of an engine and looked out to see a snowmobile glide to a stop. The rider held out a hand to his wounded partner in crime and pulled him up behind him. They sped away and Amber grabbed Lance's keys from the floor then raced to Sam. She picked him up and he struggled against her for a brief moment then let her carry him.

Lance was already at the back door. She slapped the keys into his hand. "Let's get to my car," he said. "We can head to my ranch. We'll be safe there. I have a couple of guys who work for me. They'll help watch out for us."

"First we need to get to your car."

"Follow me."

"I need to grab my backpack. And Sam's shoes."

"I'll get it. I'll throw his shoes in, too." Lance bolted to the back of the house and returned within seconds.

Amber tried to decide the best course of action. She was used to making split-second decisions when it came to her own safety, but the child in her arms brought a whole new meaning to the word *fear*. She couldn't make a wrong move when it came to protecting him. As a result, she hated to leave the security of the cabin, even as iffy as that security was, to venture into the wide-open space of outside.

But they had no choice. She followed Lance out the door, hovering over the boy in her arms. Sam held himself rigid, but didn't protest her carrying him. A fact for which she was very grateful.

Lance held his weapon ready, pointing one way, then the other. He led the way and she darted after him. She believed that the two who had been shooting at the cabin were gone, but she wasn't absolutely sure so that meant her nerves were standing on edge.

Lance didn't hesitate. He kept going through the ankle-deep snow. At least it had stopped coming down for the moment. She didn't care about the fact that they would be able to follow their prints. Not now.

"Almost there," Lance said.

Amber's arms started to ache. It didn't help that Sam began wriggling. "Down."

"Be still, Sam. Please." She huffed. She was in excellent physical condition, but Sam weighed a little over fifty pounds and conditions were working against her.

"Let me take him," Lance said.

"He won't go to you. Just keep going, okay?"

Lance didn't argue. They continued the trek with Amber anxiously watching over her shoulder. Her breath came in puffs, but she didn't stop.

They raced down the hill, along the tree line, using the trees for cover as much as possible. It felt like a lifetime, but in actuality was probably only about ten minutes before she found herself back on the road. She crossed the street and slipped into the woods. Lance led her to a small clearing where he'd pulled his Ford. Snow covered the vehicle and had hidden the tracks he'd made when he'd pulled in.

He opened the door and helped her buckle Sam in the backseat. She tucked the blanket around him and he leaned his head against the door.

The exertion had kept her warm, but now she shivered in the cold as she hadn't had time to grab her coat before bolting from the cabin. Amber raced around to the passenger door and climbed into the seat beside Sam. If someone discovered them and bullets started flying again, she wanted to be able to cover Sam with her body.

Or shoot back through the window if she had to.

Within seconds, Lance flipped on his headlights and pulled from his hiding place. "Give it a minute to warm up and I'll turn the heat on."

"That's fine." She tucked her right hand under her left armpit to warm her nearly frozen fingers. She needed to keep them limber in order to be able to pull the trigger should the need arise.

"A snowmobile picked up that wounded guy," he said. "I never heard it approach."

"They parked far enough away then walked in."

"And when the shooting started, they realized we could hold our own on the firepower. One of them went after it."

"He had to in order to pick up the guy I shot."

"Yeah."

The chains on the tires gripped through the snow and ice and Lance was able to move at a steady, if slow, pace toward his home.

"You'll need to check with hospitals nearby and see if anyone comes in with a GSW," she said.

"Yep."

She sighed. "Sorry. I know you know how to handle this."

"It's fine. You never know. You might say something I don't think of."

"Right." She looked at Sam. His eyes were open and he was taking everything in. She leaned toward him. "Sam, what is one thirteen?"

He blinked then crossed his arms across his belly and started rocking. "One thirteen."

"I know. What is it?" she pressed.

"One thirteen. One thirteen. Number One Dad. Number One Dad."

"It has something to do with your dad, huh, Sam?"

Sam closed his eyes and continued his rhythmic rocking, counting his backward and forward motion, lips moving silently. Amber knew the child well enough that pressing him now would get her nowhere. She looked out the back window and saw no headlights. In fact, the darkness of the night pressed in all around her. It made her feel safe. Deceptively safe, she knew, but for the moment, she relished it.

Then Lance was pulling into his gravel drive, the chains on the tires crunching the snow and small rocks. "I'm going to park in the garage."

"Great."

The door to the three-car garage went up and he pulled the large SUV into the space on the left. The area on the right held a boat and two snowmobiles. He shut the engine off. "Come on in."

It had been a while since Amber had seen his home. Krissy, his wife, had been alive the last time she'd set foot on the property and he'd made a lot of changes since then.

He opened the back door on Sam's side and held a hand out to the boy. Sam ignored him and climbed out on his own. Amber shrugged and slid across the seat to follow him. Sam stopped at the door and looked at his feet. Lance unlocked the door, punched in the code for the alarm then led them through a mudroom and into a kitchen. He flipped the lights on then stood still for a moment, listening. Amber did the same, her hand on her weapon.

"Alarm was armed. All looks okay. Stay here a minute."

She did and he disappeared down a hall. When he returned, he looked slightly less tense. "We're good."

"They might have seen your car. They could show up any minute if they got the plate."

"Maybe. We'll be prepared for that." He sent several texts from his phone while she looked around.

"Wow."

"What?" he asked, finally looking up.

"Your kitchen. It's really nice."

He let his eyes roam the area as though seeing it for the first time. "Oh. Thanks."

"This does not look like it used to. Did you suddenly come into some money?" She clapped a hand over her mouth. "Sorry, was that rude?"

He crossed the room and flipped another switch. The den lit up. As well as a seven-foot-tall Christmas tree in the corner near the fireplace. The lights blinked off and on, a colorful display of festivity. A stark contrast to the darkness she and Sam were battling. He turned with a small smile. "No. It wasn't rude. I did get some money from Krissy's life insurance policy, but mostly I'm just handy with a hammer and some power tools. I had a bit of time on my hands after she died." He shrugged. "I couldn't spend it all hidden away in my little cave in the mountains. Apparently, it made people worry about me."

"You still go there?" He'd always loved the caves in the hills. He knew that area better than anyone.

"Sure. It's a stress reliever for me. My get-away-from-everything place."

She scowled. "Maybe I should use it as my get-away-from-the-bad-guys place."

He smiled. "Come on and I'll show you the guest bedroom. You want to stay in the same room with Sam, I suppose?"

"Yes, that's probably best."

"All of my family lives out of town now. Dad got a job transfer a couple of years ago and my sister and her husband and kids live in Nashville. They come visit every now and then. The kids love the ranch."

"How is Janine? I heard she made you an uncle again a few months ago."

"Yep." He smiled. "That makes four for her. Two girls and two boys. She said Billy wanted a basketball team with two subs."

"Seven kids?"

"I know."

"Think they'll really go for seven?"

"Looks like it. She's homeschooling and seems to love every minute of it—even the days when she's pulling out her hair and trying to balance their finances." He smiled. "So, I know you're tired. I've got two guest bedrooms. The one at the end of the hall has its own bath. Why don't you use that one?"

"Thanks." She glanced at the clock hanging on his wall. "It's only midnight. I thought it might be two or three in the morning."

"Feels like it. Follow me."

She did and soon she had Sam tucked in. The child

was so tired he didn't have the energy to protest or oppose his new surroundings. He simply closed his eyes and fell asleep.

She heard footsteps in the hall and turned, her hand going to her weapon.

"It's just me," Lance said.

She relaxed a fraction. "Sorry."

"Your adrenaline is still racing."

"Must be."

"You'll need to crash again soon."

She lifted a brow. "Hmm."

His lips curved in a slight smile and he handed her a pair of sweatpants and sweatshirt. "The pants belong to my sister who visits every so often. The shirt is mine. It'll swallow you, but it's clean and warm. The bathroom is stocked with whatever you need."

"Thanks." She took the clothes and he stared a moment longer. She couldn't read his expression and wasn't sure she wanted to. "Is there something else?"

He started to shake his head then stopped. "You're not the same Amber Starke I used to know."

Amber let out a low laugh. "No, I'm definitely not the girl you used to know." She paused. "Is that a bad thing?"

"No. Not bad. Maybe not good either. But interesting. Definitely interesting." He turned and left, and Amber watched him disappear into the den.

Now what did he mean by that? He obviously felt the same tug of attraction she did. And while the thought was exhilarating, it was also…unnerving. She hadn't planned to be in Wrangler's Corner long, much less be attracted to a man she thought was lost to her forever. She huffed.

Who was she kidding? Romance and attraction aside,

she had killers after her. And even if she didn't, as long as she was in her line of work, she'd never get involved.

As an operative, before she had become Amber's handler just six months ago, Kat had met someone she'd thought she might be able to develop a relationship with. She'd gotten involved with a guy named Vincent Ford. She'd met him through her brother and soon found herself defending every move she made.

When she'd finally read him in, he'd dumped her. After that, Kat had wept on Amber's shoulder about having to lie about her job, her life, her…everything. She'd warned Amber to avoid romantic entanglements at all cost. Amber shook her head. She'd never met the man—Kat had been too worried about introducing him to her friends in the business. Which Amber had understood. Just one more sacrifice she'd had to make thanks to her career.

And now she found herself drawn once again to a man she couldn't have. Or at least *shouldn't* have. She groaned and sighed.

Unwilling to waste any of her remaining energy on thinking about it—or him—she looked around the room.

She needed a hot shower. She *wanted* a hot shower.

But first things first. She walked to the window to test it and found it secure. As secure as it could be, she supposed. She checked her weapon, tucked the covers around Sam a bit better then walked into the bathroom and turned on the water. While the water heated, she mulled the situation over and over in her mind.

And tried to figure out how she was going to get what she needed and get out of Wrangler's Corner without getting anyone else involved.

Or killed.

FIVE

Lance paced his large den. From fireplace to recliner where he'd start to sit then spin on his heel and cross the room again. He couldn't sit, he had to think. Backup had arrived at the cabin after he and Amber had managed to escape. He'd already reported that they were safe and in another location. The others would take care of the cleanup at the cabin while he tried to decide what to do. He glanced at his watch and grimaced. It had been a little over an hour since the attack and he needed to make some sort of decision soon.

He wanted to respect Amber's wishes that he not say anything to her family, but he just didn't see any other option. He knew it wasn't that she didn't trust them, but that she feared they'd be in danger if they knew she was here. But the very fact that the people after her and Sam knew who she was and where she lived put her family in danger.

They were going to need to bring someone else in. If they were going to live long enough to catch the people who were after Amber and Sam, they needed help. He just had to convince Amber of the fact. Amber, the girl he'd regarded as a little sister. The girl who was now an attractive woman who sent his senses spinning. What was he going to do about that?

Nothing, he decided. At least not until she didn't have killers after her. Or maybe never. He'd sworn off marriage and women in general. After Krissy's descent into her secret criminal lifestyle and willingness to kill anyone who crossed her, Lance wasn't sure he trusted his judgment when it came to women. Krissy had been immature when he'd fallen for her, sure, but when her love of money and greed for more had overtaken her, she'd stepped into crime like she'd been born to it. And Lance hadn't seen it. If he could be so blind—

He shook his head. Friendship was fine. Romance was not. However, the problem with having a friendship with Amber was that he wasn't sure it wouldn't turn into something else. And why was he even thinking about this? She had people trying to kill her. He could help keep her alive without falling in love with her.

The knock on the door sent him into the foyer. After checking out the window, he opened the door and let in the two guys who worked for him. "Hey, thanks for coming."

"Sure thing, boss, what's up?" Thirty-year-old Justin Allison pulled his Stetson from his head and held it in front of him. Handy Kilroy did the same. Handy's given name was Kevin, but he'd earned his nickname as a teenager when it was discovered he could do just about any job on a ranch—and do it well. Now Handy was forty-seven years old and a confirmed bachelor. All he was interested in was working the ranch and adding to his book collection.

Justin handled the horses and Handy worked with the dairy farm Lance had started about a year ago. It was a profitable venture and growing. Soon he'd need to hire more men, but for now, he needed to put these two on high alert. "I've run into a problem. I need you two to keep your weapons on you at all times and let me know if you see any strangers lurking about. But be careful and don't confront them, just let me know about it, understand?"

Handy's brows went up. "Boss?"

"I can't go into the details, but suffice it to say, trouble might come knocking and you need to be ready."

"All right, then," Justin said. "We've got your back."

And that was that. Lance couldn't express how much that meant to him. They stayed in the small apartment they'd helped him build at the edge of the property. A two-bedroom split plan that gave them each a bedroom and a bathroom with a kitchen and living area in between.

The two men left and as soon as he shut the door, he heard Amber's footsteps behind him. He turned and drew in a silent breath as her beauty caught him off guard. She'd changed into the sweats and sweatshirt. He decided she looked like she was about eighteen and as vulnerable as a newborn. He reined in his attraction by focusing on safety. "We've got to let your family in on what's going on."

She didn't say anything for a moment, simply stood there in the doorway looking weary—and very determined. "I'm not ready to do that yet."

"Amber, you said these guys know who you are. They've managed to follow, track or guess that you'd come here. They know who your family is. Don't you think it's the right thing to do to give them a heads-up?"

She paled and ran a hand through her dark hair. "I

wasn't planning on being here this long. It was supposed to be get in, get out."

"And then what?"

She sighed but met his gaze. Then lifted her shoulder in a slight shrug. "Then disappear forever. Or as long as it takes to keep Sam safe."

"What about the information Sam has?"

She rubbed her hands on the legs of her sweatpants. "I know. I need to get it from him. The problem is, Sam is Sam. He's special and unique and absolutely brilliant in some things. He can do math problems in his head, find meaning in numbers no one else sees. He was reading chapter books by the age of three. But I won't get the information from him by pressing too hard. He'll shut down. So until he's willing to tell me what he knows—or maybe it's not willingness, maybe it's just figuring how to communicate it to me—then I just have to be patient and pray that by the time he manages to make me understand what it is he knows that it's not too late to act on the information."

"You're sure he knows something."

"Yes. Positive. It's why his own father wants him dead."

"Then we need to bring Clay in to offer added protection—and investigative skills. He's got some high-powered law enforcement friends in Nashville, people he trusts. As highly skilled and trained as you are, the fact remains, you're only one person and you're outnumbered. You need help."

She walked over to the window and peered out. "It's dark out there. Even the moon isn't as bright as it was a little while ago."

"Snow clouds."

"I know." He could tell she was thinking. She turned back to him. "I'm not disagreeing with you. But I just don't know if I want to involve my family."

"Amber, they're already involved. These people know who you are, they know who your family is. They need protection, too. Think about what could happen if you keep silent."

She bit her lip and sighed. And seemed to reach a conclusion. "Yes. You're right, of course."

"So you'll let me call Clay?"

"Yes. Yes, call him. He can decide how much to tell and who to tell. I can't take a chance on these goons going over to my family's place and hurting them. Clay and Sabrina are living on the ranch. They built a house there last year."

"I know."

She laughed, a dry sound without any humor. "Of course you know. Aaron and Zoe are also living on the property so that should make things easier to keep an eye on." She sighed. "Seth and Tonya are on the rodeo circuit so we don't have to really worry about them, I don't think. Seth's in the top fifteen for bull riding once more so they're headed for the finals again this year. Tonya and Brady, their little boy who's what, sixteen months old now? They're traveling with him. I haven't seen Brady since he was three months old. Or Hannah, Clay and Sabrina's little girl." She sniffed and looked away. "They must think I'm the most self-absorbed, selfish person in the world. They probably hate me."

His heart ached at her pain. He'd kind of just thought she'd made her choices without regard to how her family felt. He could see that nothing could be further from the truth. She'd made her choices, but she was paying the price.

"They don't hate you, Amber. They do miss you and don't understand why you don't come home more often, but that's the nature of the job. I'm sorry that you've had to do the things you've done to protect people like me, our country. I wish you could get the credit you deserve."

She gave him a small smile. "I don't need any credit. I knew what I was getting into when I accepted the job. And I love what I do most of the time. It's had its slow moments. Even boring moments. Moments when I've been able to come home and visit family, catch up on friends." She rubbed her eyes. "I'd give anything to have those moments back right now."

"I'm sure. Hey, did you know your cousin, Becca, is back in town?"

"Really? I haven't talked to her in ages." She sounded wistful. Lance knew Becca and Amber had been tight friends growing up, before Becca's parents moved to Nashville where her father had made his first million in the banking industry.

"She's staying with your parents until the purchase of her ranch goes through."

Amber's eyes went wide. "She bought a ranch?"

"The Updike place."

"The Updike place! What would she want with that place?"

He pursed his lips and shook his head. "The Updikes decided to move closer to their grandkids. According to Becca, she wanted to move back home. She said she was tired of city life and wanted to return to her roots."

"I had no idea," she murmured. "We'll have to keep an eye on her, too."

"That's what I'm thinking."

Lance pulled his phone from the clip on his belt and hit Clay's number. A recorded message came on and he frowned. "The cell tower must be down. It's saying all circuits are busy."

Amber groaned and moved to peer out the window once more. "It's snowing out there again, too."

"Yeah, supposed to do that off and on over the next couple of days."

"Great." She started pacing just like he'd done right before she'd come in the room. "Do you have a land-line?"

"No. Just the cell."

She pulled her phone out and dialed. Listened then hung up. "I got the same message." She clipped her phone back on her belt. "I sincerely hope it's a cell tower problem because of the weather and not that the guys after us somehow managed to sabotage it."

"I don't see how they'd know which tower to mess with. They don't know where we are."

"They have a good idea of the vicinity, though."

"True."

He stood. "I've got the radio in my Interceptor. Let me see if I can reach Clay or dispatch. I need to warn them about possible strangers in town. I know it's just a week away from Christmas and there are probably a lot of out-of-town visitors, but these guys would stand out, I would think, and we need people on the lookout."

She nodded. "And if they're in town. Good idea. You do that. I'm going to check in on Sam."

Lance watched her leave, saw her roll her shoulders as she walked and figured she felt like she had the weight of the world on them right now. He walked through the den and foyer and into the kitchen where he looked around. A surge of pride hit him. It *was* nice. He smiled then opened the door to step into the garage. Once inside the Interceptor, he grabbed the mic on his radio and pressed the button to connect him to dispatch. "Gretch, you there?"

"Right here," she said, her voice crackling through. "What was going on out at the Landers place?"

"It's been a really crazy night."

"No kidding."

"I'll explain later. I'm still not sure and need to figure it out."

"Fine. What's going on now?"

He appreciated her willingness not to press the issue with questions he couldn't—and wouldn't—answer. "I'm at home right now, but I don't have any cell service out here. I'm trying to reach Clay. Can you patch me through to him?"

"Let me try."

Lance held while she worked on putting the call through. She finally came back on over the radio. "He's not answering. The call is going straight to his voice mail and he's not picking up on the radio. Want me to try someone else?"

Lance sighed. "Who's on duty tonight?"

"Ronnie Hart and the new girl, Tiffany Mansford."

Lance almost smiled at Gretchen's description of Tiffany. She'd been a deputy for almost two years now. "See if you can get one of them to run out to Clay's and tell him to get in touch with me. Then I need one of them to come over to my place. Can you make that happen?"

"I'll find a way."

"The snow is coming down again and the roads are dangerous. Tell them to use the snowmobiles."

"I will."

"Thanks." His thumb released the button, and he clipped the mic back onto the main base of the radio. He had his own snowmobiles simply because he enjoyed riding them and it allowed him to get out when the weather was bad. He hated being trapped in the house.

Last year when he'd used his personal snowmobile to get to a bad wreck that no one else could drive out to, Clay had seen the wisdom in having them as part of the department. And after one of the deputies had crashed his cruiser—in spite of the chains on the tires—on slick roads last year, Clay had organized a department fundraiser with the town's help and had raised the money to purchase the snowmobiles.

They'd come in handy twice toward the end of last year's winter, hauling those people injured in car wrecks and other winter accidents, and Lance thought it was one of the best investments the department had made. Not counting hiring more deputies for the growing town.

He went back into the house to find it quiet. Silent. At least for now. His back itched but it wasn't an itch that he could physically scratch. It was the kind of feeling that said he'd better watch his back and sleep with one eye open. All at the same time. A short time later, he heard the hum of a snowmobile outside. He pulled his weapon and gripped it while he looked out the front window. He left the porch light on and soon, the person was close enough he could make out the Wrangler's Corner uniform. Tiffany. He holstered his weapon.

"I take it you know who's out there?"

He glanced over his shoulder to see Amber standing against the wall, her weapon held ready. He nodded. "It's another deputy. I asked her to come out. I want someone else here tonight to help keep watch. Go on back in the bedroom with Sam and stay there. She'll never know you're here."

"Fine." She slipped toward the back of the house and he opened the door to wave Tiffany in. "Thanks for coming."

She took off her helmet and shook out her blond hair. Her green eyes glinted up at him. "What's going on?"

"There was some trouble out at the Landers cabin tonight."

"Yeah, I got the call and the place is riddled with bullets. You okay?"

"I'm okay. But I don't know who shot the place up. Thought it would be nice to have an extra pair of eyes tonight."

"So I'm not going to get the whole story."

"Not tonight."

She shrugged. "Fine. I can keep watch without needing to know why." She started to turn toward the door then spun back. "Whose car went over the edge of the mountain and into the ditch?"

He tensed. So they'd found it. He'd have to let Amber know. "Who did it come back registered to?" he asked with a straight face.

Her lips curved. He was as good at hiding things as she was. "I managed to use the scope on my rifle and get the plate. It's registered to someone by the name of Vivian Watson," she said. "It has California plates. Snow covered up any tracks the person made getting out of the car and up the hill. I'm thinking if it was this Vivian person, she had help."

"Really? Why?"

"That hill was mighty steep. And slippery."

He sighed. "I helped her, Tiff. I already told you that. There was an abuse situation. She's safe for now so let's just leave it at that, okay?"

"Did you bring her here? Is that why you need someone watching your place?"

He was tired of the questions. "Look, Tiff. Could you just please watch the house tonight?" He could ask Justin and Handy, but they weren't trained for this kind of thing. Having to put them on guard was bad enough. He wasn't going to ask them to be target practice for a killer. Not that he wanted to put Tiff in the line of fire either, but she was trained.

She shot him a small smile. "Sure, I'll make the rounds every so often and holler if I notice anything that shouldn't be there."

"Thanks."

"But I want the full story eventually."

"And eventually, I'll probably tell it to you."

She slipped out the door and Lance settled himself onto the couch and closed his eyes.

Amber rolled from her small section of the bed where she'd slept next to Sam. Sort of slept anyway. Sam had muttered in his sleep from time to time, but she couldn't make out what he'd been saying. Once, he'd sat up, looked at her and reached for her hand. Surprise had held her almost motionless then she'd squeezed his fingers and he'd laid back down to sleep once again.

Her heart was full this morning. Sam's small act of reaching out told her so much. He knew her and he knew she loved him and that was enough to give him comfort. She supposed that was all she could ask for at the moment. And it was enough. For now.

She slipped into the connecting bathroom and dressed in the clothes from yesterday. When she reentered the bedroom, Sam sat up and rubbed his eyes. He blinked when he saw her then looked around the unfamiliar room. His brows dipped into a frown. Amber walked over to him and took his hand. He pulled away but she didn't let it bother her. "Are you ready to get something to eat?"

"Breakfast."

"Yes."

"The Classic. Two eggs scrambled, three slices of bacon, crisp, hash browns, grits and toast. Seven dollars and ninety-nine cents plus seven percent tax in Tennessee is eight point five four nine three. Round up. It's eight dollars and fifty-five cents. Plus fifteen percent tip is twelve dollars and eighty-three cents please."

"You astound me, young man. Let's go see what we can rustle up in the kitchen." She sniffed. "I know I smell coffee."

"Coffee is extra," Sam said.

She laughed. "Yes, I'm sure it would be." She studied him. While he was in a talkative mood—at least talkative for him… "Sam, what does one thirteen mean?"

"One thirteen. One thirteen. Two forty-four. Two forty-four." He sat on the floor, crossed his arm across his belly and started rocking. "Number One Dad. Number One Mom. Number One Mom."

Amber's heart nearly split in two. Obviously, the number was distressful to him. It made him think of his parents and not in a good way. "Never mind, Sam," she said softly. "It's all right. Let's go eat. I think I smell bacon."

At first she didn't think he would respond, then he stood and walked past her and out the bedroom door. She followed him to the kitchen where she found Lance already there—and he was scrambling eggs, bless his heart. And definitely frying bacon.

Sam went to the table and sat down. Lance looked at her. "Morning."

"Good morning."

"Did you sleep?" he asked.

"Some." She glanced at the clock. "Ten o'clock. Wow. I never sleep this late."

"It was an adventurous night."

"That's one way to look at it." Not to mention the fact that was the first night in many that she'd actually felt like she could rest for an extended period of time. He handed her a cup of coffee. "Thanks," she murmured. She dumped two creams and three sugars in it and stirred. "I noticed your deputy walking the perimeter of the house a few times."

"Yes."

"I hope she didn't stay out there all night. It's freezing." Amber took a sip of the brew and felt her senses start to come alive.

"Nope, she came in off and on. We took turns watching." He met her gaze. "She knows I'm protecting someone, though, and that you're here. Well, not *you* specifically, but that someone is here. She found your car and knows that I helped the person from the car so..."

"Ah, so now she knows you brought home a stray."

"Yeah. Clay managed to get me on the radio." He nodded to the device sitting on the kitchen counter. "Several cell towers are down. It doesn't look like anything but weather related. Crews are working on them."

"That's a relief. But what'd you tell Clay?"

"I didn't give him details, just told him I needed him out at the house and that I'd explain when he got here. I also told him to put a security detail on his family's places, that there'd been a threat made and they needed coverage. Of course he wanted to know details then, but I told him to quit wasting time talking to me and to get to work on keeping his family safe. He said he would and then he'd be right over."

She frowned, but nodded. "Good."

"So, who's Vivian Watson?"

"Me. Why?"

"Tiff managed to get a look at the plates and ran them."

She closed her eyes for a moment. "Great. That's going to come back to bite me. I'm going to have to get out of here fairly quickly now. Vivian Watson is the name I used while I was working with the Pirhadi family as Sam's nanny. And that's what all the paperwork will say if anyone digs any deeper into it." She pulled in a breath. "However, it may lead my handler to my location if she gets wind of someone digging into Vivian."

"Which she will if she has you flagged in the system."

"She does."

Lance fell silent while he put food on Sam's plate.

Then he filled two more plates and handed her one. Amber placed her plate on the table next to Sam and sat. Lance set a glass of milk in front of Sam.

"Thanks," Sam said.

Lance started to ruffle the boy's hair but stopped short and pulled his hand back. "You're welcome, Sam." Then Lance sat down, as well. Sam put his fork down and looked at his food.

"What's wrong?" Amber asked him.

"Say grace."

"Oh yes, I'm sorry." She looked at Lance. "Do you mind? His mother was a Christian. She prayed before each meal when her husband wasn't around. Which was pretty often."

"Of course." Lance bowed his head.

"Thank you for this food, Lord. And please keep us safe," Amber prayed.

"Amen," Sam echoed.

SIX

"Amen," Lance whispered. He'd be the first one to admit he needed to nurture his spiritual self more. He'd been so hurt by his past that he'd simply tucked the pain away, pushed God to the side, and bulldozed on. Maybe it was time to let go of the past and start looking to the future. He let his eyes rest on Amber.

Maybe.

How had he not noticed how beautiful she was before now? While her head was bent over her plate he took in her dark hair pulled into a tight ponytail that swished with each movement. And had no trouble envisioning her sapphire-blue eyes. Both were traits she'd inherited from her father and shared with her brothers. But she was definitely a good-looking woman. He cleared his throat and tucked in to his food.

Once they were finished eating, Amber carried her and Sam's plates to the sink and turned on the faucet.

"You don't have to do that," Lance said. "I can get it later."

She shrugged. "I don't mind."

Lance's phone rang and he grabbed it. "Hello?"

"I need your credit card number, dear brother."

"Janine?"

"Are you okay? You said you were going to call me yesterday and I hadn't heard from you so—"

"Yeah," Lance said. "Right. I'm sorry. I've been a little distracted."

"With what?"

"A case. But let me get my wallet." He and his sister were going in on their mother's Christmas present. He'd agreed to put it on his card and Janine would pay him later. He reached for his wallet and patted his empty back pocket. He frowned. Then his heart almost stopped. "Ah, Janine, I'm going to have to call you back. I have to find my wallet."

"You want me to use my card?"

"No, no, it's okay. Just let me call you back." She'd already told him she didn't have any room on her credit card.

"All right then. Talk to you soon."

He hung up and swung around to face Amber. She was staring at him with a frown. "What's wrong?"

"Please tell me when you grabbed my keys, you got my wallet, too. I'd set them both on the end table when I walked in. I should have kept them in my pocket, I guess, but..." He shrugged. "I didn't." Of course he hadn't expected to get into a gun battle either.

She shook her head. "I didn't see anything but the keys on the floor." Her frown deepened the grooves between her brows. "I remember crashing into the end table and the lamp went down. We were in a huge hurry and..."

He rubbed a hand down his face. "I've got to go back to the cabin and look for my wallet. If they return to search the place, my license will lead them straight here."

"Game," Sam said. "Please."

Amber turned and frowned. "You want your game?"

"Game," Sam affirmed.

Amber bit her lip. "Where is it?" She pressed a hand to her forehead and groaned. She looked at Lance. "I think I left it at the cabin in our rush to get out last night." She pulled out her phone and handed it to Sam. "Here, use this for now, okay?"

Sam set the phone on the table and pushed it away from him. "Game."

"Come on, Sam, just play with that for now, okay?" Amber pleaded.

"No thanks. Want favorite game. Number one game. Please."

She bit her lip. Her gaze snagged Lance's. "He's not going to be distracted. If I don't get his game for him, he'll escalate into a full-blown tantrum—which is a behavior I know I need to address, but there's time for that once we're safe. Right now, I just want to keep him happy and alive." She sighed. "But, most important, we've got to get your wallet back. We can't let them find it. I'll have to go get it."

"No," Lance said. "You don't need to take a chance on someone spotting you. I'll go."

She hesitated, and at first, he thought she might argue with him. She finally gave a reluctant nod. "You're right but be careful."

"Of course."

"Game," Sam said.

Amber took his hand and Lance noticed the boy

didn't pull away from her. She knelt in front of him. "Lance is going to get it for you, okay?"

"Game's at the cabin," Sam said. "Game's at the cabin."

"I know. We'll get it."

"Game, please."

"Does he like television?" Lance asked.

"Sometimes," she said. "It depends on what's on."

Lance ran a hand through his hair then shoved his phone in his pocket. "Tiffany's gone home to rest. Clay will beat me back here."

"That's fine. I'll deal with my big brother."

"I'll try to raise him on a secure frequency on the radio and give him a heads-up that you're here."

"Sure, you do that."

"Try to distract Sam with a show, and I'll be back soon. I'll take the snowmobile." Lance grabbed his coat, gloves and hat. "Watch the windows."

"You know I will." Her hand went to her weapon and he knew she'd be on guard.

Lance walked through the kitchen door into the garage where he snagged a key from the hook on the wall. He could be out at the Landers cabin in less than ten minutes, grab the game, then be back home in another ten. Hopefully he'd be gone less than thirty minutes.

He cranked the snowmobile, pulled the helmet over his head, opened the garage and rode out. He shut the door behind him and headed down his long drive toward the road. His mind spun. He almost laughed when he thought about it. What were the odds he'd find himself in another dangerous situation?

After his dead wife's betrayal, then his friend Aaron's brush with a demented man intent on killing the woman who was now his wife, Wrangler's Corner had seen its share of evil. And Lance had been right in the middle of it thanks to his position as deputy. Now Amber had brought home another round of danger. Her family just didn't know it yet.

Which made Lance extremely glad Amber had agreed to bring Clay in on everything. He would have honored her wishes in keeping her presence a secret, but he was very worried about the Starke family. The radio on the snowmobile was connected to the Bluetooth set in the helmet. Lance pressed the button to activate it. "Dispatch, come in."

The radio crackled. "This is dispatch. Go ahead."

"Hey, Diane, I need you to patch me through to Clay."

"He's on his way to your house. You rattled him like I haven't seen him rattled in a long time."

"Sorry about that. Put me through, will you?"

"Sure thing."

After several seconds, he heard a click. "Lance, what are you doing? I'm almost to your house."

"I had to go back out the Landers place. But go on to my house and I'll be there shortly. And Clay?"

"Yeah?"

"Amber's there."

Silence for a brief moment. "Amber? As in my sister, Amber?"

"Is there another one?"

"Good point. And does the gunfire at the Landers cabin and the car that I had disconnected from the trunk of a tree and hauled up the hill an hour ago have anything to do with her?"

"Yep."

"You got some serious explaining to do."

Lance grunted. "I'm leaving that one up to Amber. See you in a few."

Clay's low growl came through the line, but Amber's brother hung up. Lance gunned the engine and leaned forward, glad that it had stopped snowing again. At least he could see through the goggles. Five minutes later, he was close enough to see the cabin. He pulled closer, parked the snowmobile next to the cabin and scanned the area. It looked quiet. Of course looks could be deceiving. He pulled his weapon from the holster at his side and slid off the snowmobile. Lance's senses tingled. The hair on the back of his neck stood at attention even as he walked toward the cabin. Yet nothing moved.

He continued his journey to the back door and twisted the knob. Unlocked. Well, they hadn't exactly had time to lock up last night. And actually, he didn't remember shutting the door behind them. There was no crime scene tape around the area, which meant the crime scene unit hadn't been there yet. Sometimes weather interfered with everything.

Lance pushed the door open with a cautious hand. When nothing happened, he stepped inside and closed the door behind him. It was cold in the cabin thanks to the broken windows but he ignored it and looked at the place where the end table was. He picked the lamp up and spied his wallet among the broken glass from the bulb. With two fingers, he grabbed it and shook it then shoved it in his back pocket. Relief filled him. Being at his home was probably still safe for a while longer. Now for the game. He moved to the hall where he'd last seen Sam with the game.

And there it was. Lance snagged it and shoved it into

his coat pocket then zipped the pocket to make sure it didn't fall out on the ride back to his house. He walked to the front door and stepped outside. Again he had the sensation of being watched. But when his gaze probed the area, he saw nothing. He walked down the steps and over to the place where Amber's bullet had found its mark. The ground was white, but he knelt and swept aside the top layer of snow. He moved methodically, in a grid-like pattern until he found what he was looking for.

Blood.

He pulled the plastic bag from his back pocket and, using a leaf, scooped some of the wetness into the bag then sealed it. The wind gusted and he shivered. Lance stood and walked around the cabin to the back where he'd left the snowmobile. Within seconds, he was back on it and headed home.

He heard the crack then felt the impact of the bullet slam into the machine.

Amber opened the door to Clay's thundercloud face. "Hey, big bro, it's good to see you."

"Really? It's good to see me?"

She stepped back and motioned for him to come inside. He did and she shut the door. "Really. I've missed you."

"You sure have a funny way of showing it. You missed Seth and Tonya's wedding. You missed Thanksgiving. You missed Aaron and Zoe's wedding and they even met because you sent Zoe here when she needed a place to stay. I can tell you missed us."

Amber sighed. She'd known this day was coming and now that it was here, she could tell it wasn't going to be any easier than she'd imagined. She was going to have to read Clay in and convince him to keep the rest of the family out of it. Clay, the big brother, her protector. And the guy who thought she was a travel writer.

"Game, Number Two Mom. Game, please."

Amber turned to find Sam pacing in front of the fireplace. She'd distracted him with a show on television about animals, his second favorite thing next to numbers. "I know, Sam, Lance is bringing it back soon, okay?"

He rubbed his head and resumed his pacing. Since that could go on indefinitely, she looked back at Clay who was staring at Sam. Then his head swiveled back to her and he lifted a brow.

"I know. I have some explaining to do." She waved him into the den. "Have a seat."

"What's going on, sis? Who's the kid? Lance called and demanded protection for the family, and I see that it's because you're in town."

She clasped her hands together and tried to figure out how she would break the news to him. "The kid is Sam Pirhadi. He's the son of my best friend. Or former best friend. She's dead."

His hand automatically reached for her. "Whoa. Amber, I'm so sorry."

She blinked back sudden tears. "I am, too. She had an aggressive cancer that she was in the US for treatment of. But that's not what killed her."

"What did?"

"Not what. Who. Her husband. He shot her in the head and I saw him do it."

"What!" Clay gaped at her. Amber almost felt sorry for him. She knew she was laying a lot on him. He had to be feeling a bit broadsided.

"And he was going to kill Sam," she said. "So I grabbed Sam and ran and here we are."

Clay shook his head as though it would help process the information she'd just laid on him. "But Amber, I… I don't even know where to start. I mean, obviously you've left out a few details so we'll come back to those, but for one, taking Sam, that's kidnapping."

"No, it's not. I have custody of him and the papers to prove it." She glanced at the backpack in the chair and knew she needed to find a safe-deposit box or something to keep them in.

"How?"

She looked at Sam again. He didn't look like he was paying attention to their conversation, but she never knew with him. She lowered her voice while Sam paced. "Sam's father never wanted him once he found out he had autism. Nadia said he was going to kill him."

Clay's jaw dropped once again.

"I know. Just bear with me. Nadia begged him not to, pleaded with him, told him to completely disown him and give her full custody. Legally. She had her own money and promised Yousef he'd never have to spend a cent on Sam. He finally agreed, but she knew if she died, Yousef would kill him anyway. Once she had everything done and in her name, she gave custody to me when she realized she was so sick. Just in case," she whispered.

"Why didn't you call or ask for help? Something?"

"Because I couldn't." She palmed her eyes then looked at him. "Clay, I'm not a travel writer."

He blinked. "What are you talking about? Of course you are. I've read your articles."

"I didn't write them, someone else did."

"What are you saying? If you're not a travel writer then what are you?"

"You seriously haven't figured it out yet?"

"Would you just spit it out already?" he half yelled. Sam jumped. Clay narrowed his eyes. "Sorry," he said in a softer tone. Sam went back to his pacing.

"I'm CIA."

He froze. His stare never wavered. "A Certified Internal Auditor?" he finally said.

Amber lifted a brow. "Really?"

"Yeah really, because the only other meaning I can come up with for that acronym isn't an option." She stared. He stared back. Finally he shook his head. "I don't believe it." She said nothing. "You're serious." It wasn't a question. He planted his hands on his hips, opened his mouth, then shut it. He rubbed a hand across his jaw and blinked again. "CIA."

"Yes."

"I...I just don't know what to say."

"I know. It's okay."

"My baby sister? CIA?"

"Are you going to keep saying that?"

"Then again, I suppose it makes sense," he said as though she hadn't spoken. "A lot of things make sense now." He continued to speak as though to himself. Like she was no longer in the room. "Could it really be true? My sister? CIA?"

Amber sighed. "Stop it, Clay. It's true."

"How... When...?"

"I was recruited in college when it was apparent I had an affinity for languages."

"How did you find that out?"

She shrugged. "I had a Middle Eastern roommate who spoke Farsi. I picked it up."

"You *picked up* Farsi."

"And you keep repeating me."

He scrubbed a hand down his cheek. "I'm sorry. You can imagine this is a bit much to take in."

"I know. I'm sorry you had to find out this way." Actually, she was sorry he had to find out at all.

The radio on his shoulder crackled. He tilted his head toward the mic and pressed the button. "Go ahead."

"Shots fired at the Landers cabin again," dispatch said. "Rachelle Michaels called it in. She was out walking her dog and heard the pops. She also reported that she saw someone fall off a snowmobile. Are you in the vicinity?"

Amber gasped. "Lance!"

SEVEN

Lance crouched behind the tree and scanned the area. The first bullet had slammed into the back of the snowmobile. The second one had puffed up ice and snow near his left foot. He'd thrown himself off the machine and rolled behind the tree where he now found himself watching for the shooter.

The bullets had come from the road, but that didn't mean the shooter hadn't moved by now. Lance gripped his weapon in his right hand and fumbled for his phone since his radio was on the snowmobile and he wasn't in uniform. He glanced at the screen of the phone. No signal. Great.

He drew in a deep breath. Now what? Wait and watch until they left. He didn't think the bullet had damaged the snowmobile badly enough that it wouldn't start. If he could get back to it, he could probably get away.

He swiped the back of his gloved hand across his goggles and squinted trying to see past the glare on the snow. The sun was high and flakes still drifted from the white sky, but nothing like last night. He finally shoved the goggles to the top of his head and snugged them up against his hat. Now at least he could see clearly.

Of course that meant he was visible to those who were looking for him, too.

Lance scrambled to his feet keeping the tree between him and the direction the bullets had come from. He moved tentatively and another shot rang out clipping the tree. He ducked back down, blood pumping in his veins. He was effectively prevented from getting to the snowmobile. He had no choice but to go on the offensive. He raced to the next tree.

No gunshots came his way.

He looked at his phone again. One bar. Lance dialed dispatch. Tessa answered. When Gretchen wasn't working either Diane or Tessa was. "Wrangler's Corner Sheriff's office."

"Tessa, I need more backup at the Landers place." He gave her the address while his heart thundered in his ears.

"I sent Ronnie out there, hon. A neighbor heard the shots and called it in."

"Is Ronnie on a snowmobile or the SUV?" Lance stared at the cabin and saw nothing. No sign of where the shooter was.

"SUV."

"Great. He's going to have a hard time getting up here."

"He's got chains."

"Let's hope that works." Lance scanned the area again. No more movement. No more gunshots. But he hadn't heard an engine start up either.

"The crime scene unit is working on getting up there today," Tessa said. "Snow's supposed to stop and the plows can get through."

"Yeah. Unfortunately, that's not helping me at the moment."

"Just stay put. Ronnie should be there any min—" The call cut off. He glanced at the screen. No signal. Lance grunted and tucked the phone back into his pocket. He wasn't waiting on Ronnie. He was going to find the person shooting at him. But was there one or two? There'd been two last night.

However, one had been wounded, which meant he probably wasn't feeling up to joining his partner in crime today. The sound of an engine caught his ear. Not one starting, but one approaching. Ronnie?

Lance bolted to the next tree and waited. The SUV rounded the curve and pulled to a stop in the middle of the road. Lance was far enough to the side of the house to see past the cabin to the front. Ronnie just sat there and he knew the deputy was assessing the situation. He wished there was some way to communicate with the man. If he rolled farther, the cabin would block Lance's view of him.

Another engine growled in the distance and Lance shot from the tree to race toward the sound. The snow slowed him. Ice crunched under his boots, but he kept going until he came to the side of the cabin. Ronnie had his door open and was stepping out when the snowmobile swept past him and disappeared around the curve. Lance bolted toward the deputy. "Get back in the car. See if you can follow him. I'm going to get the snowmobile." He raced for the machine and hopped on. He heard Ronnie leave in the SUV. Lance really didn't think they had a chance to catch the guy, but he had to try.

Amber paced the floor of the den, her movements matching Sam's earlier ones. Clay had wanted to rush to Lance's side, but Lance had convinced him to stay with Amber just in case. He had Ronnie coming and that was good enough. So Clay had stopped protesting and managed to distract the boy with a game of dominoes. Clay placed them in a pattern and asked, "How many dots?"

Sam would count them then using the remaining dominoes, pull the ones needed to come up with the same number simply by looking at the pieces. He lined them up one after the other. "Seventy-eight," he said. He tapped the ones Clay had arranged. "Seventy-eight." He looked at Clay. "Again."

Clay glanced up at her. "He's amazing."

She offered him a faint smile. "I know."

"He's adding it all in his head faster than I do."

"Yes."

"I've never seen anything like it."

She heard his incredulity, but her mind was on Lance. Ronnie had called in that he'd gotten to the cabin and he and Lance were now chasing the suspect. Or they were. Twenty minutes of more pacing and two different games dealing with numbers for Sam and Clay and she thought she might simply come out of her skin. "Where are they?"

Clay looked up. "Looking for the shooter."

"It's just the two of them. What about Joy and Parker and Trent. Shouldn't you call them in?"

"I will as soon as I know where to tell them to go." Joy West, Parker Little and Trent Haywood. All Wrangler's Corner deputies. "They're still looking for him," Clay said. He had his radio earpiece tucked into his left ear. Their conversation about her choice of occupation had been put on hold for the moment, but she knew he'd bring it up again as soon as he could. He shook his head then spoke into his radio. "Forget it. He's gone. Lance, come on back to your house." Clay's glance caught hers. "We've got a lot to talk about."

Amber wrinkled her nose at him. Sam rocked back then stood to start his pacing again. "Game."

"He's coming with it, Sam."

"Want it now! Game! Please!" His agitation worried her. She'd seen him in the throes of a fit and it wasn't pretty. Nadia had always instructed Amber to just give him the game if he got upset and it would instantly calm him. Amber hadn't had to use it often as he almost always had the game with him, but Nadia had been right. As long as Sam had the game, he was generally fine. Even more out of touch with what was going on around him, but not upset or agitated.

Her eyes roamed the area and landed on a shelf stacked with games. Old-fashioned kind. Not video or phone games. The kind Lance had probably kept from his childhood. She walked over and chose one. "Sam, let's play chess. It's a numbers game." Sort of. Didn't professionals number the pieces and the squares? Sam was certainly smart enough to learn it. He stopped his pacing at the mention of the word *numbers* and walked over to her.

"Chess. It's a numbers game. It's a good game."

"Yes." She set the game on the table and handed him the directions. "Here, use this. Read how to play then set up the board." She could have read it to him, but it would distract him and take him a little longer to do it himself. Maybe. He hesitated then settled himself in the chair to read. She should have tried all of these things before sending Lance after the game at the cabin. She grimaced. She'd panicked. She'd never had to deal with

Sam without the game. It was like his security blanket and he always had it with him and she had to admit to feeling a bit overwhelmed. Mentally, she knew that was normal. She'd gone from zero to one special-needs kid in the blink of an eye. A little panic was understandable, right? She drew in a deep breath. She could do this. She loved Sam, she'd prepared for this once they'd learned Nadia's cancer was too far spread to have much hope of a remission. She shook her head at the irony. Yousef had brought his wife to the United States to seek out the best oncologist. He would pay whatever it took to make her well. And then he'd shot her and killed her himself. She'd never understand men like him.

"What's wrong, sis?" Clay asked, his voice soft, the tenderness in his eyes making her want to cry on his shoulder like she'd done as a teen after her prom date had dumped her for another girl—and left Amber stranded at the dance. Clay had come to her rescue then, too.

The door opened and she didn't have a chance to answer. Lance stepped inside and kicked his snowy boots off in the foyer. He shrugged out of his heavy coat and hung it on the rack next to the door. His gaze caught hers. "We lost him."

"I heard. Also heard there were shots fired." She went to him. "Are you all right?"

"Yes. He got my snowmobile, though." His jaw flexed his displeasure. "Won't keep it from running, but it doesn't look pretty."

"The department will take care of any repairs," Clay said.

Lance nodded. "Thanks." His gaze darted between hers and Clay's. "So, are you two okay?"

"How long have you known she was CIA?" Clay asked. His nostrils flared and his eyes narrowed belying his calm question.

Lance blew out a breath. "Known for sure? Since yesterday. Suspected? Since she came home for Hannah's birth." Clay's wife, Sabrina, had given birth to a baby girl a year and a half ago. Amber had managed to come home and be there for that event. She'd also been instrumental in finding her sister-in-law, Zoe Starke's, brother while she'd been home. "There were several clues that I picked up on," Lance said.

"And I didn't." Her brother looked dumbfounded.

"You weren't looking for it." Lance shrugged. "I knew there was something different about her, I just couldn't put my finger on it. Then I remembered Mitch."

"Mitch?" Clay asked.

"Mitch and I were buddies in high school then college roommates. He went to work for the CIA right out of college. He had an ear for languages and they snatched him right up. He let me in on his little secret so that I could help cover for him with his family when he needed me to. Amber had a lot of the same…" He paused as though looking for the right words, "whatever…that Mitch had." He shrugged. "And I didn't know for sure, it was just an educated guess."

"Good guess," Clay grumbled.

Lance handed the game he'd retrieved from the cabin to Amber and she looked over at Sam who was engrossed in the directions for chess. He had the game set up exactly like it was supposed to be and was practicing moving the pieces accordingly. "He'll be an expert by dinner." She slid the electronic device into her pocket. "We'll use it in emergencies."

Lance nodded. Clay rubbed his forehead and looked at Amber. "So what's your next move?"

"I need to get some stuff from the barn at home and then Sam and I need to get out of here. And probably fast. Your deputy ran my plates. They'll know where I am now—or at least the vicinity. They'll probably check Mom and Dad's home first then spread out looking."

"What stuff? And who's 'they'?"

"The stuff that's hidden, but it's fake passports, twenty-five thousand dollars and some other items that will allow us to disappear. As for the 'they,' probably my handler and Pirhadi's henchmen."

Clay blinked. "Twenty-five grand?"

"Yes, it's there for emergencies." She gave him a tight smile. "I'd say this qualifies."

"So that's why you came back here," Lance said.

"Yes—and why I'm not staying."

EIGHT

Lance flinched at her words. Why, he didn't know, but the thought of her leaving didn't sit well with him. There was just something about her…something he hadn't noticed before. Truthfully, since she'd gone off to college, he'd had very little interaction with her other than a brief moment here and there. He'd always looked at her as a little sister.

But this time—

"Lance?"

He blinked. Clay was looking at him with a strange look in his eye. Lance flushed. "Yeah?"

"Are you all right?"

He cleared his throat. "Yes, of course."

"Okay, because you—"

"I said I'm fine," Lance barked.

Amber merely raised a brow then shook her head and turned to Clay. "So can you get the stuff for me and get it back to me in a hurry?"

He sighed. "I wish you'd let us help you."

"You'll be helping by getting that stuff for me."

He rubbed a hand over his head then placed his Stetson on it. "All right. Tell me where it is."

"You remember where I used to go to hide from you boys when I was around ten or so?"

"Yes." His cheeks flushed. "We teased you a lot, didn't we?"

She shot him an incredulous look. "Did you really just ask me that?"

"Yeah. Sorry." He looked down and scuffed a toe against Lance's hardwood floor. Amber knew he was remembering how insufferable they'd been to her. But as much as they'd aggravated her and teased her as a child, they'd always had her back and watched out for her, as well. Nobody messed with the Starke little sister.

"Anyway," she said, "there's a little compartment in the wall. I don't know who put it there, but I found it one afternoon while I was sulking. If you run your hand down the wall, you'll find a little knothole. Stick your finger in it and pull."

He nodded. "All right, I'll be back. You three stay put."

"Chess." Amber's gaze moved to Sam who still sat in front of the game. He looked up. "Number Two Mom. Chess. Please. Play now."

"All right." She walked to the opposite side of the coffee table and lowered herself to the floor. Lance noticed her graceful control. She didn't flop or use her hands to brace herself. She simply went down in one smooth move, tucking her legs up under her. He blinked and turned away. He didn't need to notice her gracefulness. She was leaving.

While she entertained Sam, Lance pulled Clay into the kitchen. "Your sister might be a trained spy, but she's still susceptible to bullets. I don't like the idea of her going off on her own trying to take care of Sam by herself. We need to keep her here and we need more protection around her. Although if you mention that to her, she's going to protest. Frankly, I don't want to be in the line of fire when that happens."

Clay nodded. "She's definitely stubborn and hard-headed. We'll have to think of a way to keep her here without making it obvious that's what we're doing. You know what I mean?"

"Can you delay getting those items she needs from your parents' barn?"

"I can."

Lance rubbed a hand down his cheek. "I think we're going to have to go to the top on this one. The man after her is Sam's father. His name is Yousef Pirhadi."

"Yeah, that's what Amber said."

"The people doing his dirty work are simply hired hands. Take care of them and more will just take their place. It sounds like he has quite the empire with a home in California and Ibirizstan. Amber and Sam won't be safe until Pirhadi is either dead or in prison."

"Then let's make that happen. In the meantime, I'll put out a request for help until we can catch the people after her and Sam. I've got coverage for my parents' house and the ranch, but if Pirhadi's coming after them, then we're going to need a few more guns on our side."

"Make what happen?" Amber asked. "What do you mean we're going to need a few more guns on our side? There is no our side."

"Keeping you and Sam safe is top priority," Clay said. Lance noticed how he ignored her insistence that she was going to handle this alone. "We're going to do whatever it takes to see that through."

"Right. Which is what I'm trying to do. Now if you'll

go get that stuff, we'll be able to leave. The sooner we can leave, the sooner everyone around here will be safe."

Clay stepped forward and hugged Amber. "I love you, sis."

Amber didn't move for several seconds then she hugged him back. She cleared her throat and pulled out of his embrace. "I love you, too, Clay. Now go, please?"

"Yeah." He paused yet again.

"What?" she asked.

"Glad you'll be home for Christmas this year."

Amber's jaw dropped. Clay laughed in spite of the seriousness of the situation. Lance smothered a chuckle and Amber must have heard it because she glared at him. Clay walked out the door and she turned that laser stare on him. "What were you two plotting?"

Lance put on his best innocent face. He wouldn't lie to her, but he'd do his best to dance around telling her his and Clay's conversation. "We want you safe, Amber. That's all."

She eyed him like she wasn't sure if he was telling the truth or not then sighed. "Sure. Since you're not going to share info, what do you have to eat around here?"

Amber busied herself making a snack from crackers and peanut butter. The mindless action kept her from screaming. But the busier she stayed, the faster the time would go. But it also gave her time to think. *Glad you'll be home for Christmas this year*, Clay had said.

A pang hit her. No, she wouldn't be home for Christmas this year either. She couldn't celebrate with her family because that might get them killed. Tears pricked at the back of her eyes. She ignored them and sucked in a steadying breath. Christmas music played softly in the background. Lance had tuned on a radio then settled himself in front of the chess game. He and Sam were battling it out with Lance muttering under his breath about genius kids.

In spite of her sadness over the sacrifices she'd had to make due to her job, she couldn't help the small smile that curved her lips. If it hadn't been for the job, she wouldn't have Sam. Lance seemed drawn to the child, fascinated by him, protective of him. It warmed her. She heard Sam talking and stepped to the door to listen. "One thirteen dark. Number One Dad. Afghanistan, Akrotiri, Albania. One two three."

She stilled and waited to see if he would say anything else. Lance had paused, hand hovering over the pawn he'd planned to move. His gaze flicked to hers then back to Sam who rocked back and forth, his eyes still on the game. Amber grabbed the plate of crackers and peanut butter and carried them into the den. She set them on the table next to the chess game and handed Sam one. He took a bite. "Say it again, Sam."

"Your move," he said. "Your move, Lance."

Lance glanced at her then complied. He moved the pawn forward one square.

Sam finished the cracker. "One thirteen dark. Number One Dad. Afghanistan, Akrotiri, Albania. One two three."

Amber grabbed her phone and opened the notes app. She typed in what he'd said. Then looked at it. What could it mean? She lowered herself on the couch beside Lance. His cologne tickled her nose and she breathed deep. She liked it. She liked everything about Lance.

And that was a problem. A distraction. She focused on the note in front of her. "It's like a code," she said. "He has something he wants to tell me and this is how he knows to do it. Now I've just got to figure out what it means."

"We," Lance said.

"What?"

"We. We've got to figure out what it means."

She held his gaze for a moment. "Right. We." She offered him a small smile and tried not to admit how good it felt to know she wasn't alone. Or how scared she was that letting him help was going to get him killed. Again, she yanked her thoughts back on track. She couldn't think of the possibility of Lance dying because of her. "Afghanistan, Akrotiri, Albania are all countries. Afghanistan is in the Middle East, Akrotiri is in Greece. Albania is right next to Greece, in Europe." She bit her lip and shook her head. "I'm not seeing a connection other than they're all places that start with the letter *A*." She looked up to see Sam move his knight up two and over one to block Lance's pawn from being able to take his rook.

Lance frowned. "This little guy's mind is amazing," he said softly.

"Amazing," Sam said. "Yes. I am."

Amber smiled and reached out to stroke Sam's hair. His silky strands weren't so silky anymore. "He needs a bath."

Lance looked up. "A little dirt won't hurt him."

"Don't tell me you're of the 'germs are good for the immune system' mentality?"

He shrugged. "Worked for my mother."

"Bath," Sam said and stood. "I stink."

Amber choked on a laugh. Lance couldn't smother his. "Will you let me show you where to bathe?" Lance asked him. Sam didn't answer. He just walked out of the room and down the hall. Lance looked at Amber. "Was that a yes?"

She shrugged. "Could have been a no, but you're welcome to give it a try."

Lance nodded and hurried to catch up with Sam. Amber waited and didn't hear Sam protesting Lance's help so she let herself study the couch. She wanted to take the moment to collapse on it. Instead, she pressed a hand against the comforting weight of her weapon and slipped up to the nearest window. She parted the blinds and looked out. Sunshine on the white landscape made for a brightness that caused her to squint.

Nothing moved in the distance. There were no new prints in the snow on this side of the house. She slipped into the living room and sidled up to the window to check out the front. Silence. White. Nothing that should cause the hair on her arms to stand up. Was it too quiet? Too calm? Like she was smack-dab in the eye of the storm?

She drew in a breath and rubbed her head. Clay should be back soon with the items. She needed to be ready to bolt. The problem was, she needed a car. No. She needed Lance to drive her and Sam to the nearest bus station. She started mentally mapping the route she'd take, where she'd purchase a car using her fake ID and whether she and Sam should catch a flight at an airport or she should charter a plane. She kept her gaze on the area outside the window as she worked out the details in her mind. She wasn't aware of time passing until she heard footsteps behind her.

"Sam's in the bed."

"Already?"

"He's not sleeping. I found a documentary on chess on television and he's engrossed. Is that all right?"

"Sure," she said before turning. When she faced him, she found Lance watching her with an odd expression. "What is it?"

His face cleared and he shook his head. "Nothing. Just thinking."

"About?"

"You're just so different."

"I think we've already had this conversation."

"True. I'm just having trouble processing it, I guess." He sank onto the sofa and reset the chess game.

She held his gaze. "You've changed, as well. You've been through a lot."

He shrugged. "I suppose."

She sighed and moved to sit next to him on the couch. "I used to have the biggest crush on you, you know."

He blinked. "What? When?"

"When I was in elementary school all the way up to high school. And then you married Krissy."

Bitterness flashed briefly in his eyes. "Yes. And we all know what a mistake that turned out to be."

"I'm sorry."

"I am, too. In the beginning, she was different—well, sort of. She was always a little selfish, but who isn't? Don't we all want what we want?"

Yes. She knew she did.

"Anyway, the first couple of years weren't bad. I can't say they were great, but I knew marriage was going to be an adjustment so I figured we'd hit our stride eventually." He shook his head. "She really changed when her mother got sick."

"Changed how?"

"Her mother had some money. Not a lot, but enough that she could spoil Krissy. But when she got sick, instead of buying Krissy whatever she wanted, the money had to go to medical bills. That didn't sit with Krissy and she fumed about it, even while she loved her mother and hated to see her suffering like she was."

"Sounds like Krissy was very conflicted inside."

"Very. But instead of talking about it and letting people help her, she turned inward and pushed everyone who cared about her away. Except for her drug supplier. She ran into an old high school friend one night while she was on a girls' night out kind of thing. She told him her story of woe and he offered to help her forget. The rest is history."

Amber grimaced. "I wish it had turned out different for you."

"I do, too. Some days I can't believe she's gone. Other days, it's like she was never in my life." He ran a hand through his hair. "I just knew I had to forgive her."

"Really?"

"Yeah. Doesn't mean I'll jump into marriage again, but I had to let go of the bitterness and the anger I had toward her. It was slowly killing me."

"How did you do that?" she whispered.

"It didn't happen overnight, but God—and your family—helped me. A lot."

"Oh." She paused and fiddled with the hem of her shirt then looked up at him. "I'm not real happy with God right now."

He nodded. Her statement didn't seem to faze him. "I

understand that feeling for sure." He studied her. "You want to talk about it?"

"Not really."

"Are you thinking of doing something to change the way you feel about Him?"

"Yes. I'm thinking about it," she said softly. "I believe in Him. I believe He's all powerful. I believe He's in control. So when things are out of control, it shakes that belief, that faith. All the things I've seen—and done—in the past few years…" She shook her head. "I couldn't do what I do without that belief in God, but this latest thing? Nadia's death, Pirhadi's evil? His *family's* evil. Even his brother, Deon, is involved. They're five years apart and it's like they're twins on the inside. Double the evil. It's rocked me." And, as much as she might want to deny it, it had rocked her faith.

"It feels like a betrayal?"

She froze. She really hadn't wanted to talk about it, but now that she was, it felt good to get her feelings out in the open. "Yes. And then I feel like I'm betraying God because that's how I feel."

"He's a big God. He can handle it." He gave her a wry smile. "I'm just coming to understand that in a very real way. I'm still working on my spiritual self."

She gave him a soft smile. "He's a big God," she repeated. "Sounds like something my mother would say."

"Probably where I heard it." He frowned. "My parents are good people, but not much on God and going to church. They have a passing acquaintance with Him, I suppose is a good way to describe it. I hope and pray that changes one day."

"Me, too."

"I try to talk to them when I see them. And when we

Skype, I try to tell them what God's doing in my life, but I don't get a whole lot of response about it."

She reached for his hand and squeezed it. "I'm sorry."

"Yeah, I am, too." He smiled at her and kept his fingers wrapped around hers. "But I'm not giving up on them."

"Good."

"So, anyway, you really need to thank God instead of being mad at Him."

She gave a little laugh then lifted a brow. "For what?"

"For putting me in your path when you needed rescuing."

"I didn't need rescuing," she huffed. "I could have handled it."

"Okay, if you say so." The amused doubt in his voice made her grimace.

"All right, I have to say, it turned out to be a good thing you were there when you were. Good for Sam and me anyway. Not so sure it's a good thing for you."

"Hmm. Time will tell." They fell silent then he tilted his head. "So you had a crush on me, huh?"

She felt heat invade her cheeks and gave a slight laugh even while she pulled away from him, stood and checked the windows one more time. "Yes. I got over it." *Liar.* She winced and told herself to hush. She *had* gotten over it. Sort of. He'd gotten married and that had been that. She refused to dwell on someone else's husband. And truthfully, when she was working and moving from place to place, she'd been able to put him out of her mind for the most part.

And then Krissy had died and while she'd felt awful for Lance and the circumstances around her arrest and eventual death, it allowed her more freedom to think about him. The few times she'd managed to come home, she'd found herself thinking about him constantly, wondering how he was doing, wishing she could see him—and then wishing she could be with him and—

And now look at them. She was desperate to get away from him, from Wrangler's Corner. Desperate and sad. She wanted to stay. The realization hit her hard and she let out a low gasp.

He moved to her side and placed a hand on her shoulder while he looked out the window. "You see something?"

Amber went still, his touch sending zings through her. She looked back and up. His furrowed brow made her want to smooth it. He looked down, catching her by surprise. When he did, it brought his lips within millimeters of hers. His eyes widened, dropped to her lips then back to her eyes.

Then back to her lips.

Her mind spun with options. Lift up on her tiptoes and close the gap—or run?

NINE

Lance couldn't decide whether to lean down and kiss her—or pull back and pretend he wasn't interested in doing so.

At the last second, he simply ran a hand down her soft cheek and put some distance between them. He caught the flash of disappointment in her eyes. Then something else. Maybe relief. Which was okay. He felt the same way. She was vulnerable right now. Scared, determined, overwhelmed with being thrown into the role of mother, focused on keeping Sam safe. Some bad things, some good things.

But Lance didn't need to make himself a distraction. And besides, while he might be attracted to her and want to kiss her, he wasn't interested in anything more. At least that's what he tried to tell himself.

And Amber was a commitment-with-a-white-dress kind of girl.

She blinked at him for a moment, studying his features, her own face closed and unreadable. Then she offered him a small smile and turned back to the window.

Her shoulders stiffened.

"What?" he asked.

"There are new tracks in the snow."

"Could be Trent's."

"Maybe. He's been walking the perimeter, but not coming through that area. Unless he did it and I didn't see him." She moved and pointed to the edge of the house. "See those prints? Those are Trent's." She pointed to the others. "See those? Those aren't. At least I don't think they are."

He spotted the deputy's Ford Interceptor, a vehicle that was twin to the one Lance drove, but couldn't tell if he was in it or not. This time when he leaned forward, kissing her wasn't on his mind. Protection was. "Stay here."

"Lance—"

"If Sam decides he wants you, you need to be here. Just stay put and let me do my job. Please."

Her nostrils flared and he thought she might ignore him, but she shot a glance in the direction of the bedroom then nodded. "I'll make sure no one gets in the house."

"Good."

He grabbed his coat, hat, scarf and glove for his left hand. Within seconds he was ready. With another glance out the window, he twisted the knob on the front door then slipped outside to step on the porch. He pulled the door shut behind him and simply listened while his eyes moved from one white-covered bush to the next. The trees swayed in the wind, snow falling from their branches to add to the foot already on the ground. It was warmer today, but as soon as the sun disappeared, the wet stuff would freeze all over again.

Lance liked the fact that his back was to the house, but in order to check out the footprints, he needed to move. He waved at the SUV cruiser, but didn't see Trent in the driver's seat.

Amber hadn't wanted anyone to know she was here, but he knew Clay had asked Trent Haywood to keep an eye on the place. Trent was trustworthy and could keep his mouth shut. He kept to himself and did his job. Something Lance appreciated very much. So where was he? There were no footsteps leading from the driver's side of the vehicle—at least none that he could see. Had he gotten out of the passenger side for some reason?

He walked down the steps, ignoring the ankle-deep snow. He focused on the footprints and saw that they led around the side of the house. Adrenaline rushed through his veins and his heart pounded, but he kept his movements slow and calculated, not wanting to move fast and miss something. Unfortunately, he might be making himself a target.

The wind whistled in the trees and tried to get under the scarf he'd wrapped around his neck. In his right hand, he held his weapon. The hand was bare now and would grow cold quickly, but the bulky glove would interfere with how he handled the gun. Lance had always loved the Tennessee mountain winters, even as a small child. But right now, he'd be mighty happy for sunshine and temps in the eighties.

However, he'd work with the snow, do what he had to do to keep Sam and Amber safe.

Where was Trent?

Lance, weapon held ready, rounded the corner of the house. When he saw nothing, his pulse slowed slightly.

The footsteps continued to the back porch. Lance slipped in between the bushes and pressed his back up against the house. He looked the length of his home and saw nothing but snow. Keeping his back against the house, Lance kept moving parallel to the bushes and to the footprints. Where had the person gone? He glanced at his phone. No bars, no signal. The remote location of the ranch and spotty cell service had never bothered him much before. But now he was wishing he'd invested in a satellite phone.

If wishes were nickels…

While his mind spun, his eyes never stopped moving, trying to see through bushes and trees. His ears strained to hear any sound that shouldn't be there.

And got nothing. Nothing to alarm him, nothing to say that he wasn't perfectly safe.

Except the footprints that shouldn't be there.

He scanned the tree line again, then the wide-open field to the right. He pushed away from the house and followed the footsteps to the back deck. A chill that had nothing to do with the weather swept over him. Once on the deck, there was nowhere to go but in the house. He picked up the pace a bit and stood back to look at the deck. Empty. Had the person found his way inside? No. Lance would have heard something. Amber would have signaled him somehow. So what—

He heard the swish behind him and he whirled.

Blinding pain shot through the side of his head and he spun, stars dancing in front of his eyes to see a white-clad figure bolting down the steps and heading for the tree line. Lance pressed his gloved hand to the wound and lifted his weapon. "Police! Freeze!"

The person ignored him and continued to race for the trees. Lance ran after him, his head throbbing, but not bad enough to hold him back. Since Lance had been in midturn, the blow hadn't landed as hard as it could have. And he didn't think the skin had been broken as he felt no blood dripping. The person had blended in nicely with his white storage locker on the deck. He'd have to remember that little hiding place.

His attacker arrived at the edge of the trees and stopped abruptly. His hands went in the air and he started backing up. Lance slowed, his breaths making puffs of smoke in the cold air while his head pounded in time with his heartbeat. Trent stepped out from behind one of the trees, weapon drawn and aimed at the person. "Keep your hands where I can see them. It would be a shame to mess up that nice white suit with a red stain," Trent said.

Lance huffed out another breath. "Great timing."

"Yeah. I thought I saw something and decided to see what I could find. He was watching me, trying to be sneaky."

"So that's why you went out the passenger side?"

"Yeah. Didn't want to leave any tracks where he could see them."

Lance walked up to the now-still figure and lifted a hand to pull the white mask from his face. A hand whipped out and caught him in the cheek. Pain ricocheted through him. A cry slipped out. With a growl of rage, he dove for the person and slammed him into the snow. Lance had a tight grip on the attacker's left hand while he drew back the other to land a hard blow on the white-covered face. The figure went still and Lance rolled to the left.

With his right hand, he grabbed the white ski mask and yanked it off. Long dark hair spilled on the snow and Lance jerked back with a gasp. He was a *she*. Her eyes were closed and she lay still. A bruise was starting to form underneath her eye where he'd hit her. He lifted his gaze to meet Trent's stunned one. "It's a woman," Trent said.

"Thank you, Captain Obvious," Lance muttered. "Give me your cuffs, will you?"

Trent slid them from their spot on his belt and tossed them to Lance. His gun never wavered from the woman on the snow. Lance grabbed her upper arm and started to flip her over when she burst to life once again. Her fist lashed out and caught him in the eye. She kicked out and slammed her heel into the back of his knee. Lance went down, rolled and lunged toward her.

He stopped when he saw the gun in her hand. His gaze snapped to Trent who held his gun ready, but couldn't shoot without hitting Lance. She'd maneuvered him between her and Trent. Panting, Lance lay on the ground and stared up at her. "Tell your officer to drop his weapon," she said softly. The quiet lethal tone in her voice made Lance hesitate more so than the gun that she held. He shot a look at Trent who stood still. When he looked back at his attacker, her gaze never wavered. "I'll shoot you where you are if you like."

Her cold gray eyes said she was serious. Lance nodded to Trent whose jaw tightened. The deputy's light blue eyes narrowed and he didn't move to comply. "Does he really think I won't do it?" she asked Lance as though they sat across from each other in a café.

Lance touched his aching eye. He and his attacker would have matching shiners. "Lady, we don't know you. Neither one of us know what you would or wouldn't do."

"But I do," Amber said. Lance stiffened and turned his head to see Amber standing on the back deck with her gun trained on the woman. "Put your weapon down, Kat," Amber said, "you're not going to shoot anyone today."

Kat's eyes narrowed to slits, and he hoped Amber knew the woman better than he did because as far as he could tell, she was ready to put a bullet in his brain.

"Are you all right?" Kat asked Amber without bothering to follow Amber's order to put the gun down.

"I'm fine, no thanks to you." The frigid coldness in Amber's voice said she wasn't happy to see the woman with the weapon. That coldness seeped into his bones and he shivered. "How did you find me?" Amber demanded.

"It was very simple really. I expected better of you."

"What made you turn traitor, Kat? Money? How much are they paying you to kill a little boy?"

Lance caught the brief flash of confusion in Kat's eyes. She spared a flicker of a glance at Amber before turning back to him. When she spoke, she addressed Amber even though her gaze drilled holes into him. "What are you talking about? You're the one who turned traitor. You killed your asset—the company's asset— and kidnapped her child. I'm here to take you in."

Silence. Lance swung his gaze to Amber's stunned features. Kat shot another glance at her as well before coming back to him. "What?" Amber's whisper ricocheted in the air. "Who told you that?"

Kat slowly turned her head toward Amber, but Lance didn't move. He had a feeling the woman wouldn't have to look at him to shoot him. He had no desire to find out. "It's not true, is it?" Kat asked.

"Of course it's not true. Don't tell me you actually believed it?"

In one smooth move, Kat slid her weapon out of sight underneath her white suit. Trent started toward her but Amber held up a hand. The hand that didn't hold the gun. "Don't, Trent." She lowered the weapon and motioned for Kat to come inside. "I want to hear what she has to say."

Lance rolled to his feet and glared at Kat. "Who are you?"

He heard Amber sigh. "Lance, Meet Kathryn Petrov, my handler."

TEN

Amber's nerves were shot but she kept them under control even as she held her weapon with the full intention of using it should it come down to who lived and who died. There was no way she was letting Kat hurt Lance, Trent or Sam—or anyone else for that matter.

When Kat stepped inside, Amber placed herself between the back of the house where Sam was and the woman she'd once trusted with her life. "Why are you accusing me of killing Nadia? What would even put that possibility on your radar?"

Kat stood with her back against the wall. She lifted a hand to touch her bruised cheek and shot a glare at Lance. Lance simply held her stare until she scowled and looked back at Amber. "Before I get into that, tell me why you went dark?"

Amber held Kat's gaze. "My cover was blown."

Silence fell between them then Kat gave a slow nod. "And you think I had something to do with it."

"Who else knew what I was doing? Where I was?"

Kat frowned. "Director Gideon." She shook her head. "And me. That's it."

"Then how did Yousef Pirhadi find out who I was?"

"I don't know." Her subdued tone bothered Amber. She wanted to believe Kat hadn't turned against her, been bought by Pirhadi, but she was a well-trained liar. Kat must have sensed her thoughts. She sighed and dropped her rigid stance. "Look, I found you through the vehicle. As soon as the search came back on Vivian Watson from this area, I knew you'd come home."

Amber nodded. "I thought you might."

"I was actually surprised to find you still around."

"I wasn't planning to be, but plans don't always work the way you want them to. So update me and I'll decide if I believe you or not."

"The night Nadia died, Yousef Pirhadi called the cops."

A chill invaded her and she gripped her weapon. "You can stop right there. I don't believe you. Pirhadi would never do that."

Kat ran a hand through her hair and met Amber's eyes, her gaze intense. "But he did and I can show you the police report. He claims he saw you shoot Nadia and that you kidnapped Sam. He demanded they find you immediately and get his son back. It's all over the news."

Lance crossed the room and snagged the remote from the coffee table and pointed it at the television. It came to life and he flipped the channel to national news. "We'll let it play for now and see if they say anything else."

"Great," Amber whispered. "If what you say is true, then Yousef must be desperate. He hates the cops. I can't believe he'd open his home to them, not even to investigate a crime scene."

"He didn't."

"What? He shot her in his office. In order to investigate it, they'd have to be in his house."

"She was found in her car. He's saying she was shot as she was leaving. Her body was in the driver's seat. There was blood spatter everywhere like she'd been shot. I saw the crime scene photos myself."

Amber stood still and let her brain process the information. "He faked it. Somehow."

"How many times was she shot?"

Amber frowned. "How many times? Once. A shot right to the back of her head as she was walking out of his office. She saw me in the doorway and walked toward me. When she passed him, he just pulled a gun from his pocket, lifted it to her head—and pulled the trigger." The memory flared, triggering the shock and horror of the moment. Amber closed her eyes and breathed deep.

"According to the police report, Nadia was shot twice," Kat said.

Amber blinked and forced the images from her mind that wanted to replay over and over. "So he moved her body and shot her again after he posed her in the car." Sickness rolled through her. She knew her friend was in heaven, and while that helped, she still wanted justice for Nadia. She wanted Yousef Pirhadi behind bars for the rest of his life.

"Yeah, that's what it's looking like."

Amber looked at Trent and Lance who'd been surprisingly quiet throughout the conversation. Trent caught her questioning gaze. "Nothing about the kidnapping yet," Trent said. "Are you sure?"

Kat shrugged. "If everything happened as you said

it did, Amber, it won't be long before the cops figure out it was a setup."

"He had to know he couldn't fool forensics," Lance said.

"No," Amber said, "you don't understand Yousef Pirhadi. He didn't think he could fool them, but he was probably counting on the fact that I would be captured and his son returned to him before they figured out exactly what happened to Nadia. You know how long an investigation can take and all the steps they have to follow. Yousef was probably thinking he'd be on his private plane with Sam and headed home to Ibirizstan. Where he could kill Sam without any repercussions." The words left a bitter taste in her mouth.

"It could be what you say. That he's buying himself time to get Sam and get away."

"So you believe me?"

Kat rubbed a hand down her bruised cheek. "Yeah. I do. I never really believed you could do what they're saying you did, but I had to know for sure." Her handler's eyes met Amber's. "Do you believe I didn't have anything to do with blowing your cover?"

Amber sighed. Did she? "I want to. But I don't have any idea who else it could have been. Do you have any thoughts on that?"

Kat shook her head. Her frown seemed permanently entrenched on her face. Footsteps in the hall had Kat reaching for her weapon. "Don't," Amber said. "It's just Sam."

She turned to see the little boy go into the kitchen and stand in front of the refrigerator. In Lance's open concept home, she had a good view. She started to go to him, but Lance touched her arm. "I've got him."

"Thanks."

He walked over to the refrigerator and Amber heard him murmuring to Sam. She looked at Kat who frowned. "That's Sam?" Kat asked.

"That's Sam," Amber said. How much should she tell Kat? She was almost certain the woman had nothing to do with blowing her cover, but how could she be sure? She might be willing to risk her safety, but she wasn't willing to risk Sam's.

"Tell me, Amber, I'm not the one who betrayed you."

And there it was. She'd been waiting to hear that tone. Her friend's husky voice was her "tell" and Amber relaxed a fraction. Whenever Kat was telling the truth, her voice eventually lowered slightly. She didn't do it all the time, but Amber knew if she let her continue talking, if Kat was telling the truth, it would happen eventually. Amber had never let on that she knew about the tell, so she didn't see how Kat would be faking it now.

Slightly reassured, she said, "He knows something, Kat, something he's trying to communicate and can't quite get the right words out. He had come home from school and was watching a video and I went to the bathroom. When I returned, he was gone. I went looking for him and found him in his father's office looking at the files on his desk. Notations on a piece of paper caught his attention and I had a hard time dragging him away, but Yousef was home and heading for his office. I didn't want him walking in on Sam and I didn't have a chance to look at what was on the desk. I barely got Sam out in time. I told Nadia what had happened and she said she'd see if she could get a look at what Sam had seen."

"And Yousef found her."

Amber nodded, her throat growing tight with grief.

She cleared it. "Yes. Sam went looking for her and I followed him just in time to see Yousef confront her. She gave him an excuse for being there and at first he seemed to buy it so I backed up a little. I didn't want to interfere if I didn't have to. And then as Nadia was walking out of the office, he simply lifted his arm and shot her in the back of the head." She closed her eyes against the surge of memories. "I couldn't move. I couldn't do anything. Yousef immediately turned and went to his desk to get his phone. When Nadia fell, Sam went to her and stood there looking down at her. He started spouting numbers but I can't even remember what he was saying. Yousef's face went bloodred when he turned and saw us there. He fired and hit the door frame. I pulled Sam into the hallway and waited for Yousef to come around the corner then I hit him in the throat. He went down, I grabbed Sam, the car keys and we ran."

A low hum reached her ears and Sam walked from the kitchen to the window. "Plane."

Amber rushed to him. "Yes, it's a plane, Sam, come away from the window, okay? Want to play chess?"

Sam walked into the den and sat on the sofa in front of the chess set Lance had left set up. "Seven, six, two, five," he said.

Amber blinked. Trent stepped forward. "What does that mean? Seven, six, two, five," he said.

Amber shook her head. "I don't know." She pulled the piece of paper and the small pen from her pocket and wrote the numbers down next to the notes she'd already taken about what he'd said before. "I don't know, but it means something." She walked over and smoothed the boy's hair. She smiled when he didn't pull away from her. "We're trying to figure it out, Sam. Don't give up on us."

"There. It's on," Lance said. He picked up the remote and turned up the volume on the television. A reporter spoke into her microphone and Amber recognized the house behind her. "We're here at the Sacramento home of Yousef Pirhadi, a millionaire businessman who travels frequently between his home country of Ibirizstan and the United States on business. This trip he brought his family and their nanny with him. Unfortunately, it turned out to be a deadly trip for the thirty-two-year-old, Nadia Pirhadi. She was found shot to death in her car in the driveway." Amber saw the police activity going on in the background and assumed it was filmed the day of the murder. What was that? Three days ago? Four? Time had ceased to mean anything to her anymore. The reporter continued. "The interesting thing is, we have an update in the case. The police have just revealed that Mrs. Pirhadi was shot twice, once in the car and once in another location. They've acquired a search warrant and are in the process of searching Pirhadi's home as we speak. Amber Starke, the young woman Pirhadi accused of killing his wife is still at large. Yousef Pirhadi is also nowhere to be found at this time. Stay tuned as we will be updating as we receive information."

Amber groaned and put her face in her hands. "Mom and Dad are going to be fit to be tied."

"More like worried to death," Lance murmured. "Clay will fill them in, though. He'll cover for you."

"I know, but he shouldn't have to."

Sam picked up the pawn and moved it forward two spaces. He looked up at her even though his eyes didn't make contact with hers. "Your move, Number Two Mom. Please."

With a glance at Kat, Trent and Lance, Amber moved to sit on the floor opposite Sam and the chessboard. "Seven, six, two, five," she said and moved her pawn, as well.

"Seven, six, two, five," Sam said.

"Right. So what does that mean?"

Sam knocked her pawn over with his queen. "You die."

Lance hadn't planned on having a full house, but thanks to his prepping for the snow, he had a full freezer and refrigerator. A thought occurred to him. He turned to Kat. "How did you get here?"

Kat had shed her heavy white coat and gloves and now sat in her white ski pants and pink turtleneck. Her dark hair spilled over her shoulders and Lance noticed that Trent had a hard time keeping his eyes off the woman. "I walked in."

"Where's your vehicle?"

"Parked up on a side road. The snow was melted enough for now that I could drive it. Don't worry, it's hidden."

"You didn't think we'd notice your footprints in the front yard?"

She frowned. "What footprints? I didn't go into the front yard. I came through the woods into the back and around the side of the house."

Lance froze. Amber's gaze swung to his. "But that's how we knew you were out there," Amber said.

"Number Two Mom. Your turn, your move, your turn."

Amber looked back at the board and moved then focused back on her handler. Lance's brain was already spinning with not good possibilities even as Kat shook her head. "Not my footprints, I came through the back through the trees from the road."

Trent went to the front door. "So whose prints did I see? And who was sneaking around out there if it wasn't you?"

"I don't know. I didn't see anyone else. Doesn't mean there's not someone out there, though."

"How did I miss them?" Trent asked. "I mean I got out and walked the perimeter of the house a few times, but I didn't walk up through the front yard and look around. Whoever it was should have been in plain sight."

"They were watching you," Kat said. "Waiting for you to do a round then came up through the yard. And maybe even caught sight of me."

"I didn't hear any automobiles or snowmobiles," Trent said.

Lance shook his head. "I didn't hear anything from in here either." He looked at Kat. "He must have come in the way you did. Maybe even followed you."

Kat looked like she wanted to argue. Amber simply sighed. "We need to be ready to leave just in case."

"I'll pack a bag," Lance said. "Trent, keep watch on the windows. Kat, do…whatever it is you do best as long as it involves keeping everyone safe."

Kat nodded and Amber moved another piece. Lance thought she might be closing in on Sam's king. The boy tilted his head and studied the board. Amber looked up. "We might be going at this all wrong."

"What do you mean?" Her question halted his trek

to the kitchen. He had camping supplies in his police vehicle but not a lot of food.

She glanced at Sam then Kat. "Meaning I've been trying so hard to understand what Sam is trying to tell me that I've taken my eyes off one important question."

"What's that?"

"What is Yousef's goal? What is it that he thinks Sam can interfere with? And yes, I want to know what Sam saw in his father's office, but maybe there's another way to find out."

Kat crossed her arms and leaned forward. "We need to know what he's involved with, who he's doing business with. Whom he's been talking to."

"Exactly. Nadia was giving me some of that information, but now I'm not sure how accurate it was. If Yousef suspected she was spying on him, he may have fed her false information."

"Did he suspect?" Lance asked.

Amber ran a hand over her eyes. "I don't want to think so. Of course, I want to believe we were so careful he had no reason to be suspicious until he walked in on Nadia going through his files and the information she shared with us was accurate, but now... I don't know what to believe. Nadia's dead and her husband wants to—" She broke off and looked at Sam who still studied the chessboard.

"Yeah," Lance said quietly.

Kat nodded to the laptop on Lance's desk in the corner of the den. "Do you mind? I can log in to a secure server and do some research on Mr. Pirhadi."

"Sure." He walked over and tapped the password into the machine. She slid into the chair and immediately started typing, her fingers flying over the keys.

Amber still kept Sam occupied and Trent kept a watchful eye on the windows, moving from one to the next,
his shoulders tense, his hand on his weapon, ready to
defend. Lance went into the kitchen to get the food he
wanted and set the bag by the back door. He walked into
his bedroom and checked the window. Locked, but still
breakable. He glanced out into the backyard and didn't
see anything that disturbed him. For now.

"You believe her?"

He jerked and turned to find Trent standing in the
doorway. "Sorry. Didn't mean to scare you."

"It's all right. Believe who?"

"Kat."

Lance frowned. Did he? "Amber does." He grabbed
a large duffel and stuffed a few things in it, leaving
room for some food.

"She *wants* to," Trent said.

"Maybe. But Kat was pretty convincing and I trust
Amber's judgment."

"What if she's wrong?"

Lance stopped his packing and stood still. He met
Trent's concerned gaze. "Then we might be in for a
whole new kind of trouble."

Amber glanced at the clock. Clay had been gone for
two hours now. Where was he? Sam was getting antsy,
bored with the chess game, and she was ready to give
in and give him the electronic device. She had it charg-
ing in the kitchen, but didn't think Sam knew it was
on the counter.

She walked over to check it and found it fully
charged. Then she moved to the edge of the window,
opened the plantation shutters a crack and looked out.

She saw nothing to disturb her, but somehow she knew that the people after her and Sam were out there. Waiting and watching. She closed the shutters when she heard footsteps behind her. Kat. "Hi," her friend said.

Amber nodded. "Hi."

Kat looked uneasy. As uneasy as it was for her to look. She had always been proficient at hiding her feelings, even from Amber. "Do you ever wish you hadn't chosen this career?"

Amber blinked. "Why?"

Her handler's shoulder lifted in a slight shrug. "I... just wondered."

Amber stared. "You didn't just wonder. What is it?"

Kat sighed.

"It's Vincent."

Amber lifted a brow. "Okay. What about him?"

"He came back knocking on my door about a week and a half ago."

"Really? What did he want?"

"He said he wants to try again." Even while she was talking about her personal life, her alert stance never wavered.

"What did you say?"

She shrugged. "That I'd think about it."

"Seriously?"

"But something just doesn't feel right about it all, I'll admit it."

"What feels wrong?"

Kat sighed then tightened her jaw. "I don't know. Now's not the time to talk about it anyway. I just wanted to know if you ever thought about walking away from it."

Amber hesitated then nodded. "Every day."

Sam walked up to her. "Game, please."

She sighed and handed it to him. "Okay, but just for a little while, all right?"

"Thank you."

He turned and went back to the couch where he curled up in the corner on one end, his attention already fully engrossed in the action on the screen. Lance walked in carrying a duffel bag and Kat slipped out to check the windows once again. Her friend's words echoed in her mind—and she'd probably revisit them later—but for now she watched the little boy who had her heart firmly clasped in his little hands. "I'm a terrible mother," she told Lance. "I caved."

"You're not a terrible mother. You're a great one." He set the bag on the floor and added several items to it then zipped it up.

"I've only been one for four days now."

He glanced up. "And look how far you've come." She didn't know whether to laugh or cry. His eyes turned serious, and he straightened to take her elbows in a gentle grasp. "He's alive thanks to you. That's got to count for something."

His touch warmed her, made her long for things she didn't think she'd ever have. Grief surged. Nadia had wanted those things, too, but she'd never had them. Things like a man's love and respect, a husband who put his faith in God not in the things of evil. "But his mother's dead because of me," she said softly. "I think that cancels everything out."

"She made the choice," Lance said. "From what you've told me, she wanted to do what she did. You told her the risks, didn't you?"

"Of course, but I didn't have to, she already knew them."

"And she still did it."

Amber nodded. "She hated the things he was doing, the innocent people he murdered, the pain he took pleasure in inflicting on others. She wanted to stop him. So she and Sam could be free of him. But then she got sick and she became obsessed with getting Sam away from Pirhadi." She sighed. "And we almost had him."

He dropped his hands and she missed his touch. "Why can't they just arrest him now?" he asked. "What were you waiting on?"

"Evidence. We could have taken him down with some little stuff that his high-priced lawyers would have laughed at us about. We could have even shut down his business and frozen his accounts for a while. But he never would have spent one night in prison." She shrugged. "I was willing to do it to buy time to get Nadia and Sam away from him, but Nadia refused."

"Why?"

"She didn't want to spend her life running from the man. She wanted him taken care of forever. So she could rest easy and build a life with her son. At least until she found out about the cancer. Then she just wanted to take down her husband as quickly as possible. I think it made her act too hasty—and he caught her."

"And he killed her before she had the chance to do anything else."

"Yes." She felt the surge of emotion welling up and forced it down. "So now it's up to me to make sure Sam has the kind of life his mother died trying to give him."

"Someone's outside," Trent said.

Kat rose from her seat and pulled her weapon. Lance

went to the door while Amber stayed near Sam, ready to sweep him into her arms and cover him if bullets started flying.

"It's Clay," Lance said.

The tension in the room deflated, and Amber wanted to wilt. Her adrenaline had been fired way too many times over the last few days. In her line of work, she stayed on guard and tense most of the time, but at least there had been times she'd been able to get away and be alone. Just her and the beach or her and the gym. She'd found ways to combat the stress of the job. But now it was all built up inside her and she was afraid she might explode if the situation didn't end soon.

She heard Clay's heavy footsteps on the porch and then Lance was opening the door to let him in. Clay stepped inside and shut the door behind him. Her gaze snagged his. "Did you bring it? The stuff I hid in the barn?"

"Couldn't find it."

Her heart fell. "What?"

He shook his head. "I couldn't find that little hiding place you were talking about. It's not there."

Amber wanted to hit something. A wall, her brother... She drew in a deep breath. "All right. I'll just have to go get it myself."

Sam walked over to Amber and put his face in her stomach. Just like he used to do to his mother on a pretty regular basis. But he'd never done it to *her*. Even when she'd been with him day in and day out, he'd reserved that affection for his mother. She swallowed the tightness that gathered in her throat and put her arms around the child. Just like his mother used to do. He sighed and stood still. He might not be able to show it like other six-year-olds, but he needed comfort. He needed to know it was going to be okay. "Don't worry, Sam, it's going to be fine. You'll see."

"One thirteen dark," he mumbled against her stomach. "Number One Dad. Afghanistan, Akrotiri, Albania, Algeria, American Samoa, Andorra. One, two, three, four, five, six. Seven, six, two, five."

Amber went to her knees and tried to look into his eyes. He was trying so hard to tell her what he knew. "Afghanistan," she whispered. "Akrotiri, Albania, Algeria, Amer—" She looked up at Lance. "Countries of the world. All *A*s. He's naming them in alphabetical order. What's one thirteen?" Excitement zipped through her. Had she finally figured out what Sam was telling her? "Come on, someone. Look it up, please?"

Lance pulled out his phone and gave a grunt. "No signal but my Wi-Fi is still connected." He tapped the screen. Amber waited. Lance finally looked up. "One thirteen is Ibirizstan."

"And what's two forty-four? He mentioned that number, too. Back at the Landers cabin."

"The United States," Clay said. She shot him a look and her brother shrugged. "Just a guess."

Lance nodded. "Great guess. Two forty-four is the United States. What are seven, six, two, five?" He looked at his phone again. "Angola, Andorra, Akrotiri, American Samoa." He sighed. "It makes no sense. Now they're out of order."

Amber turned back to Sam. "What does it mean, sweetheart?" she whispered. "What does it mean?"

A loud crack then the explosion of glass filled the air.

ELEVEN

"Get down!" Lance hollered and tried to get to Amber who had Sam already on the floor, shielding him with her body. The boy screamed and struggled against her.

Amber held tight and maneuvered Sam under the coffee table. She bumped it and the chess game flew off. Ignoring it, she pushed the table up against the couch with a protesting Sam under it. She stayed at the opening so Sam was effectively trapped under the table and up against the couch. He screamed and kicked and added his displeasure to the chaos. Lance saw that she had him safe, if not under control. She was talking to him in a low voice that wasn't having any impact at all. At least not that he could tell, but at least the child was safe from the flying bullets.

Clay was already at the window, weapon aimed. He fired. Two more shots and more breaking glass.

Lance stayed low and went to the other window. He glanced out and saw two snowmobiles and two long-range rifles resting on their seats and pointed at his house. The attackers were using the snowmobiles as cover. "You see them, Clay?"

"I see 'em."

"I've got the back of the house," Kat said. Kat raced toward the back of the house, her weapon drawn.

"I'll get the other windows in the kitchen," Trent said.

The bullets stopped for a moment and silence reigned. Lance took a peek out the window and saw the two shooters aiming their weapons behind them. Movement behind the large barn alerted him. "There's someone else out there."

"Who?" Clay asked and stepped up look out.

"I don't know, but I don't think our attackers expected them. They've turned their weapons away from us and are aiming at the barn." Lance drew in a breath. "It could be Justin and Handy. They were probably home and would've heard the shots. I warned them trouble might be coming."

"Hope they stay out of sight."

"Yeah."

"We can't assume it's them, though."

"I know."

One of the shooters kept his weapon trained behind them, the other turned to aim back at the house.

"Keep them occupied while I get Amber and Sam out of here."

"How? The temps are falling again. Where will you go?"

"I have a little hideaway place up where the caves are." He had to raise his voice over Sam's angry screams. "It's not bad, better than camping and I can keep us warm and fed."

"How will I find you?"

"I have a radio up there. You can find me."

Clay picked up his own radio. "Where's that backup?"

"Ten minutes out," came the crackling reply.

Lance checked his weapon once more. "It's snowing again. Hopefully it'll be enough to cover our tracks."

"No," Clay said, "you need to come to the ranch. I've got help coming to watch it."

"Are they there yet?"

"Not the complete group. This weather is playing havoc with travel." He scowled. "But there are enough out there to keep you and Amber and Sam safe."

"No," Amber said from her position under the coffee table. She dodged a foot to the face. "I won't take danger to Mom and Dad. Forget it."

Lance thought he heard Clay growl. The man was definitely frowning. "Fine. But I need someone to go after. I need a name, an organization."

"You have it," Amber said. "Yousef Pirhadi."

"Come on, Amber, I know that. I need a back door. Someone who'll help me get him." She hesitated. "Who?" he pressed.

"There might be one man. He works for Pirhadi and he's no innocent by any means, but he didn't seem quite as hardened as the others."

"A name."

"I know him as Taj Melbourne."

"There's no one out back that I can see," Kat said as she walked into the den. "Just the four in the front and they've stopped shooting for now, but Trent is keeping an eye out in the back just in case they decide to move that way." She went to the window nearest Lance. "Are they still out there?"

"They are. But they haven't sent any more bullets flying this way and that makes me nervous," Lance said. "I think two men who work for me are out there and sent a few bullets their way as a warning to cease and desist. For now, they're not moving. It's like they're trying to figure out their next move."

Sam's screams ceased almost as abruptly as they'd started. Lance looked to see Amber still under the table with Sam. Only instead of fighting her, Sam had his head on her leg and was rocking back and forth. "We're going to walk out of here and let Clay and Trent cover us," Lance told her. "Are you up to it?"

"We're going to the caves?" she asked. A trickle of sweat dripped from her temple and she swiped it on her shoulder. Sam had given her a workout.

Lance nodded. "It's the only thing I can think of for now. The bad guys don't know about it and we'll be safe there while Kat and Clay do some more investigating into Pirhadi. Backup is on the way out here, but I don't know how long it's going to take them to get here thanks to this weather. The hike won't take long. Thirty minutes at the most. I can carry Sam if he'll let me."

"We could take your snowmobiles," she said.

"And Pirhadi's goons would follow us right to the cave. The snow will cover our tracks faster than it will the snowmobiles'."

Amber hesitated then swept Sam's dark hair from his forehead. He felt warm and his chest rose up and down with his rapid breaths. He watched them with distant eyes, but he *was* watching and listening. "Yes, you're probably right. All right. We'll need supplies."

"Already packed them just in case."

She nodded then looked down at Sam. "We're going to get dressed up very warm and then we're going to go on a short hike, okay, buddy?"

"I have a smaller coat he can use. It's one my nephew

uses when he comes to visit. It'll still swallow him, but it'll keep him warm."

"Good. That'll work," Amber said.

Kat turned from the window. "They're leaving."

Lance heard the hum of the snowmobiles—and the sirens in the distance. "They're leaving, but they'll be back."

"I think I might have had something on Pirhadi before the attack," Kat said. "Looks like he's done some extensive travel outside of Ibirizstan and met with some shady characters."

"Shocking," Amber muttered.

"But I can't place him anywhere he shouldn't be without good reason. He owns several businesses and travels to them frequently. He does other stuff while he's there. Stuff that looks like not-so-good stuff, but still…he has a reason to be there."

"Keep looking."

"Ravi," Sam said. "Ravi, Ravi, Ravi."

"Who's that?" Kat asked.

"I don't know," Amber said and crawled from her tight spot. She stood and helped Sam up. "But see if you can connect a person named Ravi to Pirhadi. At this point, anything is possible."

The sirens grew closer. The hum of snowmobiles filled the house. "Plane," Sam said.

"No, those are snowmobiles, Sam," Amber told him. "Now we're going to get going while there's no one out there to shoot at us."

Amber bundled Sam up so he could barely see through the small crack between the hat and the scarf across his face but she didn't want him getting cold.

Once they were ready, Lance threw the duffel bag on his back and led the way out the back of the house. Clay would take care of the officers that had arrived on the scene and make sure evidence was efficiently collected. Anything he needed analyzed would be shipped to the lab in Nashville. In the meantime, she and Sam and Lance would be on their way to safety.

It was cold. The temperatures probably hovered in the freezing range. "Watch out for ice," Lance said.

"Yep." She held Sam's hand and he let her. He was probably totally confused, but at least he was calm for now. And hopefully warm enough. Amber tucked her chin into her borrowed scarf and couldn't deny that in spite of the circumstances, it felt wonderful to have one of Lance's heavy coats surrounding her. It made her feel close to him. She'd always thought her friends were silly when they would wear their boyfriends' letter jackets and jerseys. She'd never had a boyfriend— they'd all been too intimidated by the Starke brothers. It wasn't until she was in college that she'd finally been able to breathe—and have guys notice her without fear of being interrogated by a Starke male.

But she'd never worn one of her boyfriends' coats. Amber followed in Lance's footsteps and decided she just might not give the coat back. Assuming they came down from the caves in one piece.

Sam seemed to like the hike and if Amber hadn't been concerned about feeling a bullet strike her between her shoulder blades, she would have enjoyed it, as well. However, she really just wanted to arrive at their destination and hunker down until she could figure out their next move.

She looked back and saw that Lance's house was a good distance away. "Not much farther," he said.

The exercise was keeping her warm, and soon she was ready to shed the coat she'd only a few minutes before decided she never wanted to part with.

Sam stopped and sat down. Lance looked back, over their shoulders, then again to her and Sam. "What's wrong?"

"I'm not sure. He's probably just tired." She tugged on his hand. "Come on, Sam, it's not much longer. I'll carry you." She picked him up and he laid his head on her shoulder.

Lance tucked his weapon away and held out his hands. "Let's see if he'll let me carry him."

Amber hesitated, but knew he'd have more stamina than she at this point. "All right, but give me the duffel bag." Lance set the bag on the ground. Amber passed Sam to Lance and the child did the same thing. Simply laid his head on Lance's broad shoulder. She frowned and decided to count their blessings at his lack of a protest.

She drew her weapon and stayed behind Lance and Sam, her adrenaline rushing. And while they now had some tree coverage, she still didn't like being out in the open. She picked up the bag and slung it over her shoulder. Lance continued to lead the way, up the hills and through the snow. He knew exactly where he was going so that helped make the short journey a bit easier even though the snow continued to fall and she knew soon it would be to her shins. But at least their tracks would be covered. And Sam appeared to be content to let Lance carry him.

Lance gave a grunt. "Here we are."

Amber blinked. "Are where?"

He smiled. "At my favorite place." He reached out and it looked like he was going to try to push over a tree. Instead, he reached past the trunk and she heard a low hum start. It was faint, very quiet and she probably wouldn't have noticed it if not for the situation. Sam lifted his head from Lance's shoulder and pushed the scarf off his face.

Lance walked around the tree and disappeared into a small crack in the rock barely wide enough to let him through. Amber followed him and blinked, hardly able to believe her eyes. Two small lamps glowed in what would have been darkness. A love seat sat against one wall, a bookshelf was on the opposite one. A recliner faced her. A coffee table sat in the middle of a rug. "What... When... How?"

"And I have electricity thanks to a generator."

"The hum I heard."

"Yes."

She looked up at the ceiling where he'd installed a vent. "And that's why I feel warm air blowing in here."

"Yep." Lance set Sam on the twin bed at the back of the cave and handed him his game. Then he walked back to the opening and pulled a piece of plastic over it. He turned to her. "After Krissy's betrayal, it was hard to stay in the house, but I didn't want to move. That was my land, my family's land." He shrugged. "But I needed a place to go to...heal, I suppose. I used to take long hikes, spend all my spare time up here when I wasn't working. And one day I came across this small cave. It's very small and there's only one way in and one way out so not very good in a sense that if we get caught here, we're sitting ducks."

Her eyes roamed. "It looks like a small apartment. You framed it and drywalled it and everything. And this floor… Wow. I love the hardwoods. I'd never believe we were in a cave—except for the lack of windows."

He gave a nod and tilted his head toward the back to the little door next to the bed where Sam lay still. "There's even indoor plumbing—rustic, but it works."

"Amazing. And you did all this by yourself?"

"Yes. This is my therapy." His lips quirked up in a half smile. "It was cheaper than a psychiatrist."

"Wow. When you said you were handy with a hammer, I never imagined."

"It would never meet code with a building inspector, but it's something I worked on while I dealt with my anger and bitterness toward Krissy—and God. And now I come up here when I just want to get away or think or whatever."

She bit her lip. She could understand the bitterness, the anger. She was working on some of that, as well. "Did you ever feel like God let all that happen as a punishment for something?" she blurted. "That all the bad things happened because—"

He lifted a brow and she looked away, biting off her words. Sam had fallen asleep on the bed, his game beside him.

"You mean like because I wasn't good enough or because of some of the choices I've made along the way that might have not been the right ones and God decided to put me in my place so to speak?"

"Something like that," she murmured.

"No." She let her gaze collide with his. "That's not His nature. At least I don't believe that. We need to have a healthy fear of God, but not a fear that stems from worrying about 'if I do this, then God's going to strike me down' kind of thing. Yes, He allows us to have consequences, but—" He shook his head. "I'm not explaining this very well, but here's what I've come to understand. There are consequences for our actions. Natural consequences. If I speed, I might get stopped and get a ticket. If I put my hand on a hot stove, I'm going to get burned. If I marry someone my parents and friends warn me about then I might end up a very unhappy man. But not because He deemed it necessary that I needed to suffer because I was 'bad.'"

"Your parents and friends didn't like Krissy?"

"No, not really." He sighed. "I couldn't see it at the time, but they all said she was using me."

"For what?"

"To get out of her home. She had a lousy home life."

"I remember hearing that. I also remember she was really pretty."

"Yes." His mouth gave a wry twist. "And I'm ashamed to say that that's pretty much all I saw until after I said 'I do.'"

"I'm sorry."

"I am, too. And truthfully, it wasn't just that she was pretty. She paid attention to me, she made me feel like I was her hero and that I could do anything."

Amber studied him, saw a flash of self-loathing. "She did that on purpose and you fell for it?"

"Yeah. She played me like a piano. I was so gullible. And now she's gone, and all I feel for her is…nothing. Or maybe pity. I hate that she was so unhappy that she felt she had to look for contentment in drugs and crime. And of course, there's regret that I refused to listen to those who knew her better than I did." He shrugged.

"But I don't miss her and I don't think God made her do what she did so He could punish me. We were created to have free will. Krissy made her own choices and as a result, there were consequences. Those consequences affected me. The same is true of me. I made my choices instead of listening to those who were wiser than me and I suffered the consequences. But it wasn't God out to punish me."

Amber stared at him as he spoke, his words resonating within her. She knew he was right. She'd grown up in church, listening to the Word and reading it on a daily basis. Until she joined the CIA. Then she'd let herself become consumed with the job, with doing whatever it took to ensure she handed out justice to those who deserved it. Perhaps God didn't hate her, maybe He wasn't mad at her. It could be she was just suffering the consequences of the choices she'd made. But she'd done good work, made the world a safer place for everyone including her family. But still…it was something to think about.

Lance continued to look at her, his eyes…weird. Tender? "What?" she whispered.

He blinked. "I just…" His hand came up and cupped her cheek.

She swallowed even as her heart thudded. "You just what, Lance?"

"Probably should take a look outside." He leaned back and disappointment hit hard.

"Sure. You do that and I'll make sure Sam's comfortable."

He nodded, but seemed reluctant to be the first one to move. So she pushed down the desire to fling caution to the wind, wrap her arms around him and kiss him silly. But as he said, there were consequences to every action and she wasn't sure she was prepared to deal with them.

While Lance peered through the heavy plastic over the opening, she walked over to check on Sam. It was now warm in the cave and he didn't need to be all bundled up. She gently removed his scarf and coat, then pulled off his gloves. He felt hot to the touch. She frowned and slid a hand down his long-sleeved shirt to press it against his back. Also hot. "I think Sam might have a fever."

Lance looked back at her. "Could it be because he was all bundled up?"

"Maybe. Come feel."

Lance stepped to the bed to press a hand to the child's forehead. Sam muttered something and rolled to his side. Lance let his hand fall away and looked at her. "I think you're right."

Fear struck her. She knew it was irrational. Kids got sick all the time and in a few days they got better. But how was she going to take care of a sick child and keep him away from the people who wanted him dead?

TWELVE

Lance looked over to see Amber sitting on the bed next to Sam. He thought she'd dozed off for a while. But over the last thirty minutes, every so often she would reach out and touch Sam's forehead. "I've let Clay know where we are," he said.

"How?"

He pointed to the small table in the corner near the "door." It held a device that he didn't think she'd noticed up to this point. "Police radio."

Her eyes widened and he held up a hand. "Don't worry, I used a secure frequency. We deputies often need to talk among ourselves so we had to have a way to do that without worrying about outside ears." He shrugged. "I wanted to be away from everything and everybody, but I didn't want to be stupid. Cell phone service up here stinks. Clay and I had already been using the frequency to talk earlier so we just stayed on it."

"I heard you talking, but didn't realize what you were doing. What did Clay say?"

"Said they were still looking into the information we gave them including the name Ravi."

"Good."

"He also said they ran the blood I collected at the Landers cabin through the federal DNA database."

"Did they come up with anything?"

"A fellow by the name of Sebastian Wyatt."

She frowned. "I don't recognize that name. Do you have a picture?"

"They're still searching for one. Apparently he's managed to stay off the radar."

"I see. What about Kat? Anything from her?"

"Clay said she might have something, but didn't want to say what until she was sure."

She grimaced and felt Sam's forehead again. "He's getting hotter, not cooler. I need to give him some ibuprofen."

"Do you have any?"

"Yes, there's a bottle of children's ibuprofen in my backpack. Please tell me you grabbed it."

"It's in the duffel."

Relief crossed her face. "I was so worried about getting Sam out of the house and to safety I didn't even think about the backpack. It has all of his papers in there, too."

"I figured you might want it." He pulled her backpack from the larger bag, set it on the sofa and opened it.

"Second section," she said. "I just dropped it in there."

He found the bottle and popped the lid. "Two?"

"Yes. Sometimes he'll take them and sometimes not."

"Grape flavored. I might like a couple myself." He tapped two of the chewable pills into her outstretched palm.

"Thanks." She turned to Sam and rested a hand on his thin shoulder. "Hey, buddy, I need you to wake up and take these."

Sam ignored her. She sat him up anyway. He grunted and pulled away from her then lay back down on his side. She sighed and dropped her head. "It's no use trying to force him. The last time he was sick, he refused to take the medicine and his fever shot up. Fortunately, Yousef was away on a business trip and we were able to get him to a doctor. Sam had to be hospitalized for strep for two days in order to get the medicine in him. They had to sedate him," she said softly and brushed her hand across the boy's head again.

"Why did Yousef have to be away?"

"He wouldn't have allowed Nadia to take him to a doctor."

Lance frowned, a dangerous anger at Pirhadi taking hold of him. "I'd like to punch him. A lot."

"Get in line," she murmured. She pressed the heels of her palms to her eyes. "This could make a bad situation even worse. If I can't get this medicine in him, we'll have to get him to a doctor."

Lance pursed his lips and rubbed a hand over his jaw. "We'll do whatever we have to do. Let's get creative."

"What do you have in mind?"

"I've got nieces and nephews. My sister bribes hers sometimes."

"That won't work with Sam."

"But he likes numbers."

"Yes."

Lance sighed. "We could turn it into a game, but I'm not sure that would be a wise thing to do. He could get ahold of some medicine in the future and take it, thinking it was part of a fun game."

Amber gave a slow nod. "I see what you're saying." She glanced at Sam. "His fever is at least 102. He has all the symptoms he had before when he had strep. The way he's clutching his stomach in his sleep and wanting to drink to soothe his throat. If we don't get some medicine in him soon, we're going to have to take him to a hospital."

"There's a new hospital just outside of Wrangler's Corner. The growth around here has been crazy."

She nodded. "Okay, that's a positive. The hospital is nearby. However, the negative is, so are the bad guys."

Sam sat up and rubbed his eyes then touched his throat. "Drink, please. Water. Hot." He whimpered.

Amber shot a desperate look at Lance. "Let's play the game. I'll just have to lock up any medicine in the house for a while." She grabbed the cup of water from the small end table next to the bed and handed it to Sam. He drank it slowly, grimacing with each swallow. Amber snagged the medicine bottle and tossed it to Lance. "Do your thing."

Lance hefted the small bottle then sat on the bed next to Sam who took another sip of his water. "Sam, how many milligrams are in each pill in this bottle?"

Sam blinked. Lance held the bottle out to him. Sam frowned and took it. He read, "Each pill contains 100mgs."

Lance opened the bottle and dumped the remaining pills into his left hand. "Count the pills, Sam."

Sam did. "One, two, three, four…" All the way to sixteen.

"What're the total milligrams?"

Sam looked away then back. "Sixteen times one hundred is one thousand six hundred milligrams."

"Eat one pill, Sam."

Sam did. Lance breathed a sigh of relief. "What's left?"

"One thousand five hundred."

"Eat another pill and tell me what's left."

Sam ate the second tablet. "One thousand four hundred milligrams."

Lance capped the bottle. "Sam, only eat two pills every six hours." Sam held out a hand. "Two every six hours. What time is it?"

Sam looked at his electronic game that also had the time on the front screen. "Four o'clock in the afternoon. Two pills every six hours. Two pills at ten o'clock nighttime. Tired." He lay down, rolled on his stomach and closed his eyes.

Amber let out a slow breath and Lance caught her eye. She gave him a teary smile and sniffed. "Thank you," she whispered.

He shrugged. "It worked this time. But if it's strep— and I suspect you're right—he'll probably need an antibiotic. Strep can have serious complications." He studied the now-sleeping boy. "Not that he'll develop them, of course, but if we can get him an antibiotic, he'll be better off."

"I know."

"I'll radio Clay and see if he can get one and bring it up here. Is Sam allergic to anything?"

"No, nothing." Then she scowled. "And tell Clay not to let the bad guys follow him this time."

"I'm pretty sure I won't have to recommend that."

"How are my parents?" she asked softly.

"They're fine. There have been no attacks or anything on the ranch or anyone associated with it."

She pursed her lips and nodded. "It's because they know we're not there."

"Meaning they're still watching my place."

She nodded. "I imagine they retreated somewhere in the hills and were watching us walk away from your house. Now they're just biding their time until they can come this way and look for us. They'll be well armed and traveling by snowmobiles. In theory. I don't know that for sure. Except for the well-armed part. *That*, I'm sure of."

"I'd say it was a good guess."

"Kat will be watching," she murmured. "I imagine Clay will be, too."

He tilted his head. "Maybe," he said. "Probably." He stood. "You hungry?"

"Yes." She glanced at Sam. "I should try to get him to eat something like some soup, but if his throat hurts as bad as I suspect it does, he'll not want anything."

"I've got a microwave, but I don't want to cook anything that will smell and lead someone to us. At least for now, even though they might know we're up here somewhere, they don't know *exactly* where."

She nodded and sat forward. "Radio Clay and tell him to get a team of officers together and keep an eye on this area."

"You think they'll try something."

"The more I think about it, the more I do, but I also think we're pretty safe and well protected here." She looked around. "I mean, there aren't any windows and there's only one way in and out. They can't burn us out or shoot us—"

"Could gas us."

She grimaced. "But hopefully they won't have that kind of equipment, but if they do, we'll just have to hope Clay and the other deputies can cover us."

"Where would they get the snowmobiles?" he asked.

"They're not going to want to rent them in town, it would set off too many alarms. Think they'd chance bringing them in by truck with this weather?"

"I don't know. They could steal them or have them brought in by a chopper." She bit her lip and looked over at Sam who still slept. "I just wish he was somewhere safe, away from everything that could happen and everything that could go wrong."

Keeping Sam safe was her priority. But how could she do that when they were constantly looking over their shoulders? While Lance explained their thoughts and the need for an antibiotic to Clay via the radio, she paced the small confines of the little room, stopping to check on Sam every so often. He didn't feel near as hot as he had an hour ago and she was relieved, but knew that his fever would spike again in a couple of hours.

They were going to have to leave. She had to get him medical attention. But if they left and the hit men were watching, would they be killed before they could reach the hospital?

She ran a hand through her hair and massaged her scalp as she debated her options. Unfortunately, there weren't many.

And tomorrow was Christmas Eve. She let her fingers smooth Sam's silky hair and wondered how much he understood about Christmas. If he knew that he was special and wonderfully made just as he was. On that note, she hoped he never understood that he was considered "different" and just continued to be the great kid that he was. *God, I know I haven't been talking to You as much as I should have these past few years. I'm thinking that was a mistake. I'm sorry. I want to believe that You're not punishing me by letting Nadia die. I want to believe that what Lance said is true. Show me, please.*

She drew in a deep breath as she let the prayer flip through her mind. She meant every word of it. She wanted to believe that God wasn't sitting up there just waiting for her to mess up, but loved her like her own father did, with patience, kindness—and forgiveness when she needed it.

She left Sam sleeping and walked over to sink onto the sofa next to Lance.

Lance touched her shoulder. "Are you all right?"

She swiped a tear she hadn't realized that she'd shed. "Yes, just thinking about what you said earlier. About God. About choices and consequences."

"And?"

She shrugged and shot him a small sideways smile. "I told God I wanted it to be true."

"It's true."

His absolute certainty touched her. "Thanks, Lance."

"For what?"

Amber let out a little laugh. "For everything. For this. For putting your life on the line and not letting me go through this alone. I'm still determined to leave if we have to, but I'm praying Clay and the rest of us can get Pirhadi without having to do that." She wrapped her fingers around his. "You were right about that, too."

"What?"

"The fact that if we run, we'll be running forever." She drew in a deep breath. "I think it's time to stand and fight."

"I think you're right." Lance leaned over and kissed her. Amber froze at the feel of his warm lips on hers. How often had she thought about this moment? Dreamed about it? Begged God for it? At first, she wasn't sure what to do. She'd kissed and been kissed in the past, but this was…special. This was Lance. She gave a small sigh and let him pull her closer, his warmth covering her, surrounding her, making her feel safe.

But she wasn't. And she needed to remember that.

She leaned back and looked into his eyes. "Why did you do that?"

A flush covered his cheeks. "I wanted to." He cleared his throat. "I'm sorry. It was probably not the wisest thing to do."

"I don't know about wise, but I enjoyed it." She heard the wryness in her voice, and he gave a small chuckle. "However, you're probably right." His chuckle faded and she sighed. "Getting emotionally involved wouldn't be smart. Once Pirhadi's out of the picture, I've got a job to get back to."

She wanted to stuff a sock in her mouth. *Getting emotionally involved? Really? That's the best you can come up with? It was just a kiss, Amber, not a marriage proposal.*

Lance blinked and cleared his throat. "Of course."

Restless, a tad embarrassed, Amber went to check on Sam. And frowned. He was hot again. She looked back over her shoulder. "We need to get him to the doctor. The ibuprofen didn't last long enough."

Lance nodded. "I'll tell Clay the situation's changed and he needs to bring us transportation."

"I really think so. Sam's getting very lethargic." She pressed an ear against his chest and thought she heard some wheezing. "I'm worried it might be something more than strep." She hesitated. "They could be watching Clay, waiting for him to make another move so they can follow."

"I'll tell him to be prepared for that." Lance got on the radio and she heard him telling Clay what they needed. He looked up. "He's already on the way and he's got a snowmobile in tow."

"Hopefully that's the only thing he's got behind him," she murmured.

"Yeah."

She packed what little she'd removed from her backpack in the short time they'd stayed in Lance's little hideaway. She was loath to leave it and she knew it was because she felt safe here. But it wasn't long until she heard the hum of a snowmobile. Lance went to the entrance and she stepped up behind him. He rolled the plastic away from the door and the cold air rushed in. She shivered, but ignored the chill. "Can you tell if it's Clay?"

"It's him."

She stepped out of the cave and waited for her brother to pull up. Relief swept over her when she saw what he drove. A snowmobile that would seat three and another in tow. She could sit in the seat and hold Sam while Clay drove and Lance would drive the other one. Perfect. "I'll get Sam."

She went back into the warmth of the cave and touched Sam's shoulder. Heat radiated from his small body. "Hey, buddy, we're going to ride on a snowmobile and get you to the doctor."

He moaned, but rolled over to look at her. Her heart cramped. *God, please let me do the right thing. Help me help him.* She picked him up and he laid his head on her shoulder. She grabbed the heavy coat he'd worn from Lance's house and threw it over him. It was big enough that it covered him from head to toe. She'd use it to keep him sheltered from the wind.

"You got him?" Lance asked.

"Yes. Let's go."

They walked out to Clay who waited with the snowmobiles running. He wore a ski hat and goggles. Sam lifted his head as she climbed into the backseat of the machine. The coat fell from his head and he ducked back under. She strapped them both in and nodded to Lance who'd climbed on the other snowmobile. "Let's go."

A shot rang out and pinged off the roll bar of the snowmobile. Amber's adrenaline shot up as she hunched over Sam and made them as small as possible in the metal seat. "Clay!" If a bullet hit the back, they would be protected. If it came from the side…

"Hang on!" Clay called. He gunned the motor and slid the snowmobile into the copse of trees just around the side of the cave that had sheltered them. The cave wasn't formed right inside the mountain, but rather jutted out with the opening at the side. It made the mountain look like it had a swollen area jutting from it. However, the shape of it made for a flat area beside it before sloping upward. Clay pulled into that flat area, utilizing the cave for protection on one side, the slope provided some cover on another side. However, the top of the cave could be an issue should someone manage to climb up there. Lance pulled in behind them. Clay jumped off the snowmobile, his weapon in his hand. Lance did the same.

He looked at her. "Stay put."

And really, there was nothing else she could do. She would stay hunched over Sam until someone shot her or they were able to get away.

She raised her head slightly and saw Clay hovering at the front of the snowmobile. Lance covered the back, his weapon swinging from the upward slope to the top of the snow-covered cave. "They've cut their engines," he said.

"They're going to walk in," she said then looked up. "Or come at us from above. Be ready."

She heard Clay on the radio asking locations of the other deputies, and she hoped they would arrive in time to help fight off the attackers, but she wasn't going to count on it. She slid Sam onto the seat and he lay across the two like a bed, his eyes closed. Good, his back was protected, but she felt him shivering even under the heavy coat she'd wrapped him in. Chills from the fever. She pulled the hat off her head and pulled it over his. The temperature hovered just above freezing, but as the sun fell, it would get colder.

Amber pulled her weapon and held it steady, her eyes dancing between the areas beyond Clay and Lance. Movement behind the tree nearest Lance captured her attention. Did he see it?

He raised his weapon. She did the same. The figure rounded the edge of the tree pulling the trigger. A hail of bullets peppered the back of the snowmobile and she ducked even while she fired back.

Another round of bullets came from the other side of the cave. She looked at Clay and he caught her gaze. "Backup."

"They got here fast."

"I had them follow me and come in from different directions. We should have them surrounded."

"Smart."

Another bullet came from the hill above her and puffed up the snow behind the snowmobile. She spun and aimed in the direction the bullet had come from but held her fire. She wouldn't shoot blind. She heard the snowmobile behind her roar to life and Lance pulled it up next to the one where she and Sam were. From her position on the floor, her views of the hill area above were completely blocked.

And so was the shooter's.

Another shot sounded and Lance dove from the machine to the ground. "Lance!" she cried.

"I'm not hit," he answered back. "Just trying to make sure I stay that way."

Her heartbeat doubled and she swallowed her relief and fear. More gunfire came from the other side of the cave and she figured the Wrangler's Corner deputies were doing their best to subdue the attackers. She heard a cry and another shot. How many were there? Two? Three? More? Who had been hurt?

Amber glanced at Sam and worried about his stillness. He was still breathing fine as far as she could tell, but she wanted him under a doctor's care ASAP.

She lifted her head in time to see Lance bolt from his cover. A white-clad figure rounded a tree and Lance slammed into him before he had a chance to pull the trigger. They went down together, wrestling. Lance's gun spun from his hand, a hard fist landed on his face and he cried out. Lance's weapon lay too far from him to reach, but he couldn't have gone for it even if he'd been able to grab it.

He had one gloved hand wrapped around a black-clad wrist and was desperately fighting to keep the attacker from aiming his weapon at him. In a smooth move, he managed to roll the man to his back. Still keeping a death grip on the man's wrist, Lance locked his legs against the man's stomach, and landed a solid punch to the attacker's jaw. The man simply grunted and struggled harder. Lance lost his grip on the wrist, the gun leveled on his face. Amber took aim and without hesitation, squeezed the trigger. The man under Lance jerked. Lance grabbed the weapon from the suddenly slack hand and rolled off. He stayed low, keeping the gun turned on the bleeding man who gripped his shattered arm and yelled obscenities at Amber. Lance's gaze flicked to Amber who met his eyes. "Thanks," he huffed.

"Anytime." She ducked back down and turned to find Clay missing. Where had he gone?

She didn't want to leave Sam alone so she bit her lip and waited.

The shooting had stopped, but the chaos hadn't. Clay came back around to her side of the snowmobile. "We've got 'em."

"All of them?"

"All but one," he grunted. "There was one who got away. Ronnie's gone after him."

"Great."

Clay looked over her shoulder. "Need any help with him?"

"Sure," Lance said. "You can have him."

Clay moved to take the swaying prisoner from Lance. He cuffed him ignoring the man's cry of pain when he pulled his injured arm behind him. "Shouldn't have decided to come shooting if you don't want to accept the consequences," Clay growled. He yanked off the ski mask. "You know this clown?"

Amber stared into a familiar face. "He's Pirhadi's right-hand man," she said. "His name is Roger Quinn."

"You're a spook," Roger growled.

"And you're a killer," Amber said without emotion.

"Pirhadi and Deon don't like to lose," Quinn said. "They won't give up."

"I'll be ready." She nodded to Clay. "I'm done with him."

"Plane," Sam whispered.

Amber spun to find Sam looking at Clay's hat. It had a plane on it. One of the more popular airlines that he flew when he had out-of-town business. She went to Clay and gathered him to her. "Yes, it's a plane."

"Plane." Then he sighed and closed his eyes once again.

"Lance, you take that snowmobile and get Sam to the doctor. We've got these guys covered. There were four," Clay said to Amber. "We'll find out who they were working for and get information from them."

"We know who they were working for."

"Yeah, well, it'll help coming from them." He looked at the man Amber had shot. "There'll be paperwork for you."

"I know."

"We'll take care of it later. Get to the hospital."

Lance climbed on the snowmobile and cranked it. Amber tucked Sam against her once again and belted them in then looked around. "Where's Kat?"

Clay shook his head. "I don't know. She disappeared a while back."

Amber frowned, but nodded. "All right. We're ready."

Lance nodded and soon they were moving quickly down the mountain with one of the deputies following. She thought it was Tiffany. She knew why Clay had sent her. Because one of the attackers had gotten away and Clay was probably concerned that he would try something again.

Amber figured he was right and kept her gun close.

THIRTEEN

Lance paced the tile floor of the hospital room and Amber leaned her head against the back of the chair. Tiffany, the deputy Clay had sent with them, guarded the door. Thanks to Tiffany and Lance's presence, they'd been ushered directly to a room in the Emergency Department where the nurses had done their best to make Sam comfortable while they waited for the test results to come back.

The child's fever was lower, and he seemed to simply be sleeping. Lance walked back to the window.

"You can sit down, you know."

Amber's quiet voice filled the room. Filled his head. He turned to see her leaning forward in the chair, smoothing the hair on Sam's forehead. She did that a lot. A gesture of affection. Love. And it hit him that she was now a package deal. Whoever wound up with Amber would wind up with Sam. A six-year-old autistic boy who would need specialized care the rest of his life. Lance swallowed at the thought.

"Hey, you okay?"

He realized he hadn't responded to her. "Oh, yeah. I'm fine." But was he? He wouldn't deny his interest in Amber. He wouldn't deny he wanted her to stick around so they could see if there was anything to pursue in the way of romance after all this was over. If it was ever over. He rubbed a hand down his face. What was he thinking? He sighed. What he'd been thinking ever since he'd seen Amber when she'd come home for the birth of her niece. That he wanted to spend time with her.

Well, he'd gotten that, hadn't he?

Not exactly like he'd imagined, true, but the time had still been…telling. Like telling him he hadn't imagined that she'd been attracted to him the last time he'd seen her and that the feelings were mutual. Telling in that he never really knew her at all. And now someone was trying to kill her and she had a six-year-old son. Yeah. It had been telling all right. Was he man enough to deal with her and Sam? To be what they would need him to be? And why was he even thinking along those lines? She didn't plan to stay in Wrangler's Corner and he wasn't leaving.

"Lance."

He blinked. "What?"

"You have a really strange look on your face. What are you thinking about?"

He tried to relax. "Keeping you and Sam safe. Making sure you get to live the life that you deserve. That you both deserve."

She frowned. "You're being weird."

"Sorry." He forced a smile.

A knock on the door brought instant relief from the awkward conversation. Lance crossed the room and opened the door. Dr. Daniel Cullen stepped inside. "How's he doing?"

Daniel, a friend of Lance's from high school, walked over to look down at Sam. Lance cleared his throat. "Why don't you tell us?"

Amber studied the doctor, anxiety written all over her.

Daniel smiled. "He's going to be fine. He's a sick little guy, but he'll recover in a few days. He's definitely got strep so we're treating with that." He tapped the IV pole. "There's a bit of a sedative in there, as well. From what you said—" he shot a pointed look at Amber "—about his last hospital experience, we don't need him pulling out his IV."

She grimaced and nodded. "That's probably the best thing for him."

"And, he has the flu."

"What? The flu, too?" She gaped and Lance frowned.

Daniel nodded. "Unfortunately. We'll keep him here overnight for observation, but he should be fine to go home in the morning. As long as you can get the medicine in him."

Amber looked at Lance and shot him a soft smile. "I think I know how to do that now."

Lance's heart thudded. His shoulders straightened. He almost shook his head at his reaction. Honestly, he couldn't let her have that silly effect on him.

"Have you two had your vaccine?"

"Yes, I have," Amber said. "But so did Sam."

"It happens. Hopefully, the vaccine will make it a lighter case. So," Daniel said, "we'll call it a night. If you need anything, just buzz the nurse." He glanced at the whiteboard on the wall. "Deborah's on tonight. You'll like her. She loves working with the children—and she's good at it."

"Thanks so much."

He nodded. "And Lance, it's been a while. You plan on coming back to church any time soon? We've missed your sharp wit in small group."

Lance gave a low chuckle. "You mean my sarcasm?"

"Okay. That."

"I hope to be back soon. Tell everyone I said hello."

Daniel left with promises to do so. Lance heard the door shut and turned to find Amber's gaze on him. "You go to a small group?"

He shrugged. "Yes. When I'm not working."

"Or rescuing CIA operatives and their child?"

"Exactly." He turned serious. "Thank you for today."

Her eyes didn't leave his. "You're welcome."

"He got the upper hand," he said softly, loathing to admit it.

"I know."

"I'd be dead if you hadn't shot him."

"I know that, too." She blinked. "Let's not rehash it."

He walked over and cupped the back of her head. "Amber, I—"

"I'm not staying in Wrangler's Corner, Lance, I have a job to do."

He stiffened, but didn't pull away. "And how does Sam fit in with that job?"

She blinked then sighed. "I don't know yet."

"I think you do."

"What do you mean?"

He opened his mouth to speak then simply leaned over and kissed her. Just like last time, she went still then slid her hands around his waist and kissed him back. He felt her desperation and her conflict in the kiss. She wanted to stay, but felt she had to leave. He didn't want her to go, but didn't know what he'd do if she stayed.

Because he wasn't ever getting married again. He pulled back. "I'm sorry."

She simply looked up at him then nodded and turned away to walk over to Sam's side.

"Amber—"

Another knock on the door interrupted them again. Lance's hand went to his weapon then relaxed a fraction. Tiffany wouldn't let anyone in who shouldn't be let in. He went to the door and opened it. Clay stood there. "Hey, come on in."

Clay, still dressed in his winter snowmobile clothes, had fresh flakes on his hat and coat.

"I guess it's snowing again," Amber said. Her voice sounded steady, and Lance wondered if the kiss hadn't rocked her quite as much as it had him. The thought pained him.

Clay brushed at the white stuff. "Yeah." He looked at Sam. "Is he going to be out of here for Christmas?"

Amber nodded. "Yes, from what the doctor said, he just needs rest and meds. He can do that at home." She frowned. "Wherever that winds up being."

"At the ranch, of course."

Amber sighed. "Not if I've still got killers after me. I won't take that chance. Mom and Dad have already been through so much, I won't add to it."

Clay's mouth tightened, but he didn't argue with his sister. Lance figured she hadn't heard the end of it, though. "Did you get anything from the men you caught shooting at us?"

Clay rolled his eyes. "Not a lot. They're a tight-lipped bunch. But it's because they're scared."

"Terrified, probably," Amber said. "Pirhadi won't take their failure well."

"He was with them," Clay said.

"What?" Amber straightened.

"We got him on a camera in town in the back alley of the sheriff's department."

Amber stared and her jaw dropped slightly. "What was he doing back there?"

"Probably watching for me. If he knows who Amber is, it's highly likely he knows who her family is. And what we do for a living. He might have figured that I'd be the one she'd come to for help since I'm a cop." His jaw flexed. "And I didn't see him. We got a complaint from the café next door that there was arguing out back. By the time Parker got back there, they were gone."

"Or hiding," Amber said. "But he doesn't do his own dirty work. He has millions of dollars. He pays people to kill for him."

"Well, this time he's involved."

She gave a slow nod. "Well, this time his son is involved, and that might make a difference. And he's got an ironclad excuse to show up here. He can be the outraged, grieving father personally searching for his kidnapped child."

"But with the papers you have," Lance said, "it proves he's not quite the grieving father. He signed his parental rights away to his wife."

"Yes, but if I'm not alive to produce the papers then…" She shrugged.

"Right."

Sam turned his head and sighed. His eyes flickered, opened and landed on the hat in Clay's hand. "Plane."

Clay looked at the hat. "You like the plane? You want to go flying on one when you're better?"

Sam yawned, then coughed. "Plane's coming. Dangerous Ravi."

Amber leaned forward. "What?"

Sam sighed. "Plane's coming." He closed his eyes and drifted off again.

Amber tried to make sense of it. "He said there's a plane coming and Ravi is dangerous."

"Well, those weren't his exact words," Lance said, "but I can see how you might translate it that way."

"Or he could just be thinking about something he saw on television. A show with a person named Ravi who was dangerous. I don't know." She rubbed her eyes.

He placed a hand on her tense shoulder. "Do you believe he's trying to tell us something?"

She paused, as though wanting to be sure of her answer before giving it. She looked at Sam. "Yes. Yes, I believe it."

"Then let's take what he's giving up and put it together."

"But how?"

Lance took Clay's hat. "For one thing, he's fixated on planes. He's mentioned the word several times."

Amber sucked in a breath. "Seven, six, two, five," she whispered.

Now it was Lance's turn to frown. "What?"

"What if it's a flight number?"

Amber stood. "And it's coming from one thirteen to two forty-four."

"From Ibirizstan to the US," Clay said.

"But there would be connections. There's not a direct flight from there, I wouldn't think."

"And which flight is he talking about? I imagine there are several flights a day with that flight number."

"If it *is* a flight number," Clay said. He pulled his phone from the clip on his belt. "One way to find out."

While he searched, Amber stretched. Fatigue pulled at her. Lance's phone dinged and he checked it. After reading the text, he looked up. "That was Ronnie. He's at the jail."

"And?"

"He said they had to bring one of the prisoners here to the hospital. He took a bullet to the chest. They hauled him on the snowmobile as it was faster than trying to get an ambulance out there. Trent's with him here at the hospital."

Amber straightened. "Is the prisoner awake?"

Lance shot a text to Trent and Amber waited, her heart thudding. This might be the break they needed. His phone pinged again. Lance read then looked up. "Yes. Kat is with him, as well. Trent said she showed up a few minutes ago. The prisoner's getting ready to go back to surgery, but says he needs to talk. To you."

"Me?"

Another sound from his phone. "Trent said if we want to get anything out of this guy, you're going to have to get it."

"What's his name?"

Lance texted. His phone dinged again and he looked at Amber. "You know a guy named Taj?"

She froze for a split second. "Yes, I know him. He was often the driver for us when Nadia, Sam and I would go into town or wherever Nadia needed to go.

Sometimes she went and I stayed home with Sam. He didn't seem that loyal to Yousef, but I could never get him to talk to me."

"Sounds like he might be ready now."

She stood. "I'll go to him. Where is he?"

Lance frowned. "Not alone, you're not."

"I'll take Tiffany with me. She could probably use a break. Clay can watch the door for a little bit while you stay in the room with Sam." She itched to move, to pace and think. To get some answers from the man with a bullet in him. "I'll be right back."

"Aren't you worried about someone you know seeing you?"

"No." She reached into the backpack she'd managed to grab in all the chaos and pulled out a pair of black-rimmed glasses, a baseball cap, makeup and a hair tie. Then she went to the mirror and used the makeup. Within seconds, she'd transformed herself.

Lance blinked and his jaw dropped. "If I didn't know it was you, I'd never look twice. That's amazing."

"We learn all kinds of cool things in spy school. I'll be right back."

Clay nodded, his brow furrowed. "As long as Tiff's with you. When you get back I'm going to head over to the jail and talk to our prisoners one more time. I want to present this new information to them, tell them Taj talked and act like we know what's going on. See if that shakes anything loose."

Amber nodded. "Good idea. Wish I could join you."

"You just keep that little boy safe. I'll keep you in the loop."

"Fair enough." She stepped out of the room and Tiffany turned. "Would you like to take a walk with me?"

Amber asked her. "Clay's going to keep an eye on the door so you and I can go visit someone." Clay had finally introduced her to Tiffany at the hospital when he'd had the deputy cover the door. Amber figured there was no sense in trying to keep her presence in Wrangler's Corner from law enforcement. Not at this point. She did not want, however, to be recognized by anyone else.

Confusion flickered in her eyes, but she shrugged. "Sure."

After a quick stop to the ladies' room around the corner, they headed for the elevator that would take them down to the second floor where surgery was located. Amber was anxious to speak to the man, but didn't want to hurry. She wanted to watch her back. "We're going to talk to one of the men you captured out at Lance's ranch. He's heading for surgery and is insisting on speaking to me before he goes under."

"Good, maybe you'll learn something."

"That's the hope," Amber said. She flicked a glance at the deputy. "How long have you worked in Wrangler's Corner?"

The pretty blonde smiled. "I've been here a little over two years."

"You like it?"

"I love it. I'm a small-town girl at heart."

"Where are you from originally?"

"Manhattan."

"I knew that wasn't a Tennessee accent."

The elevator dinged and the doors slid open. Tiffany stepped out, her hand on the weapon at her hip. Amber wasn't comfortable with the deputy being right at her side. She stood out like a sore thumb, but Amber hoped her disguise was good enough that no one would realize who she was.

"Hey, Tiff, how are you?" A young woman rushed up and gave Tiffany a hug. Amber slowed her pace, but kept going, not wanting to be seen with the deputy and raise questions. Tiffany seemed to understand. Amber heard her say a few kind words, offer to pray for her friend's father, then excuse herself.

Amber let her gaze touch on each face she passed. She didn't know how Pirhadi could possibly know they were at the hospital, but she wouldn't assume he didn't. He seemed to have eyes and ears all over town. She felt sure he knew that one of his men had been shot in the raid and would be taken to the hospital. She wouldn't put it past him to show up. From the corner of her eye, she saw Tiffany coming up on her left. "There's a coffee bar. I'm going to get some." She didn't necessarily want coffee, but it would give her a chance to scan the area without looking like she was doing so.

"That would be wonderful."

She went to the window and ordered. Tiffany did the same and Amber paid for both. While they waited for the coffee, she again studied the faces around her. Her tension eased slightly when she didn't recognize anyone—and no one recognized her. "All right, let's go see what Taj has to say."

Together, she and the deputy walked down the hall to the surgery center. Amber paused at the door and scanned each face. There were twelve people of various ages sitting in the chairs. Two children played in the small area loaded with toys and books to her left. No one paid any attention to her so she approached the waiting area desk where a gray-haired woman named Eve—

according to her silver-plated name badge—seemed to be the one in charge. "I'm Amber. I hear you have a patient who's asking to speak to me."

Eve looked over the top of her glasses. "Oh yes. I was instructed to bring you right back. Follow me, please."

Amber did, her gaze roving, nerves twitching. Tiffany followed a few steps behind. Once they were through the secure doors back where they held patients for surgery, she was able to relax a fraction. Eve led them to a room closed off by a yellow curtain. She poked her head inside. "She's here." She then gave a little wave and headed back toward her station.

Trent stepped outside and motioned her in. "Wait here," she said to Tiffany. "Watch everyone walking by. If anyone hesitates near this room, will you let me know, please?"

"Of course." Tiffany planted herself just outside the curtain where she would have a good view of anyone coming or going.

Amber stepped inside the curtained room and noted the nurse to the side, the doctor with the chart and the patient in the bed and Trent keeping watch over his prisoner. The doctor looked up with a frown. "We really need to get him into surgery. He's already lost a lot of blood."

"Hopefully this will just take a minute."

Trent waved her forward. She stepped up beside the dark-haired, dark-eyed man on the gurney. His eyes were closed. She touched his arm and his lids fluttered. "Taj, talk to me."

He raised a hand and pulled the mask from his mouth. "Yousef…"

"Yes?" She leaned forward.

"He's here."

"I know. Why does he want me dead?" Taj's eyes closed again. She nudged him. "Come on, Taj, you need to get that bullet out. Talk to me."

The man looked at her through slits. "Don't let him kill Sam."

"I'm trying to keep Sam safe, I promise." She had a vision of Taj pushing Sam on the swing in the backyard before Yousef had yelled at him to get back inside and leave his "imbecile" son alone. She'd seen the flash of fury in Taj's eyes before he'd left Sam to her and hurried back to the house.

"Ravi…"

Amber sucked in a breath. The name Sam had used. "Yes?"

"On the plane. They're coming with a virus."

"What kind of virus?"

"Go," he said. "Watch for Yousef. I set you up… s-sorry."

"How did Pirhadi find me, Taj? He knew I was here."

"Sam's shoes—a tracker—your handler's—" He let out another labored breath and shuddered. Then fell unconscious.

"All right, that's it," the doctor said. "We're going to surgery." He nodded to the orderly who moved to grasp one end of the gurney.

Before she could blink, they were out of the room and rolling down the hallway. Tiffany looked at her and raised a brow. Amber's gut twisted. She hadn't missed a tracker on the car, she'd missed it on Sam. She pulled her phone from her pocket and texted Lance. Get rid of Sam's shoes. There's a tracker in them. "Well, I know how they've been finding us this whole time."

Doing it now. Lance's text came back almost immediately.

She had to get to Sam. They needed to move him ASAP. She turned back to Trent. "Where did Kat go?"

"She said she had some arrangements to make and she'd be in touch."

"Thanks." Amber headed for the elevator. "What did the prisoner have to say?" Tiffany asked as she fell in line beside Amber.

"The same thing Sam did. Only Taj said something about a virus and a setup, but I'm not sure how to put it together to make sense. He also said something about..."

"About what?"

"About someone I thought I trusted, but now I'm just not sure." *Your handler's*— What had he been trying to tell her? How did he know Kat? *Did* he know Kat or just that she had a handler?

Tiffany frowned. "That doesn't sound good."

"No." Her phone buzzed and she glanced at the screen even as she debated whether or not it would be faster to take the stairs. "Lance texted me. He said there's definitely a flight with that number from Sacramento to Atlanta, but it was also a connection from Ibirizstan. The last leg of the flight is supposed to land in New Mexico."

"Then that's where the meeting place is. So someone needs to intercept the passengers on that flight when it lands."

She texted Lance back. Check the manifest. See if there's a man by the name of Ravi on board.

Already done, Lance replied. There was. But they changed their itinerary at the last minute and are on a plane set to land in Nashville.

They're meeting here! Because of Sam.

Looks that way. Plans are being made for law enforcement to greet the passengers coming off at the gate. They'll apprehend this Ravi and take him in for questioning with a minimum of fuss.

Taj mentioned a virus. Tell them to be careful.

She let out a slow breath. "So, that's it for now. I need to get back to Sam."

She and Tiffany returned to the elevator to wait. The blond-headed doctor to her right studied a legal pad, his head bent, gold-framed glasses perched on his nose, stethoscope wrapped around his neck. He tapped something into his phone.

The elevator doors opened and the fire alarm went off. Red lights flashed, the sound was deafening. Amber spun and saw people standing in brief confusion before heading to the exits.

"I've got to get to Sam!" She raced for the stairs, Tiffany behind her. She flung open the door only to be greeted by a flood of people coming down. Going against the flow of the traffic, Amber pushed her way up. She had to get to the fourth floor. In her mind, she knew Clay and Lance were watching over Sam, but her heart was screaming at her to get to him. Her phone vibrated against her hip and she grabbed it. A hard hit to her elbow caused the phone to fly from her grasp and hit the step in front of her.

She grabbed for it when something jabbed her in the side. She looked to see the same doctor who'd been standing beside her waiting on the elevator. His hand gripped her upper arm. "What are you doing?"

"Shut up. Do as I say or your pretty bodyguard will die. I'm not here alone. Pirhadi just wants his son." Tiffany had stopped to help an elderly woman up who'd fallen on the stairs. Her distraction had enabled Pirhadi's man to act. Pirhadi had probably set it up and pushed the poor woman. "Move," he said. "Take me to Sam."

"No."

"Do it or I blow up the hospital. You understand?"

She hesitated, torn between believing he really had the capability to do something like blow up the hospital and getting Tiffany's attention. Tiffany looked up and caught her eye. And Amber realized she had no choice. She had to respond as though the threat was real. Amber motioned she was going to get Sam. Tiffany frowned and shook her head.

The gun pressed harder and she continued to weave in and out of the thinning crowd. The fact that Pirhadi had one of his men make a move in a crowded hospital was a testament to his desperation.

Tiffany fell behind.

"Get out here," the man said. At the second-floor landing, she pushed the door open. He kept the weapon steady against her. "We're going to change stairwells."

"He's probably not even there," she said. "They've most likely evacuated him with the others."

"He's still there." He tapped his ear and she noticed the earpiece for the first time. "I haven't heard otherwise. Now move." He ground the weapon in her lower back and she bit her lip against the pain.

Chills enveloped her. He had someone watching the room? Amber let him direct her down the hall while she searched for a way to get away from him without putting anyone else in danger. She saw nothing she could do and frustration bit at her. The only thing she could do was take them to Sam. Once they entered the room, she would twist in front of the gun and take the bullet, praying Lance and Clay would be able to subdue the man before he could fire again. Her plan set, she said a prayer, placed herself in God's hands and headed for the room.

FOURTEEN

Lance hung up and tried Amber's number again. The fire alarm continued its assault against his ears. He wanted to go find Amber, but wouldn't leave Sam alone. He knew she'd want him to stay, but it took everything in him not to walk out the door. Clay was on his phone, commandeering his deputies and giving orders.

He peered out the door and saw the empty hallway. Sam's IV still dripped healing medicine into his small body and he slept through the noise and the chaos thanks to the sedative in the bag. "Why isn't she answering?"

Clay looked up. "This fire alarm isn't a coincidence. Something's going on. I reported the possibility of a virus on the plane coming in. Kat texted me and said she'd gotten TSA involved as well as the FBI and other antiterrorism agencies."

"Good."

A hospital worker poked his head in the door. Lance's hand went to his weapon and he noticed Clay's did, as well. "Who are you?"

"I work here. We need to get you out of here. It looks like a fire broke out in the bathroom down the hall.

There's smoke coming out around the door so we're not opening it. We'll need you to leave. There are workers who can direct you to a safe area of the hospital. Fire trucks are on the way."

Clay held up his badge as did Lance. "We're staying right here. Just forget you saw us."

The man's eyes went wide. "But the fire…"

Lance and Clay didn't move or speak.

"Right." The worker spun and disappeared.

Lance shook his head. "Will you stay with Sam while I go look for Amber?"

Clay hesitated and Lance decided to take that as a yes. He slipped out the door and heard Clay's too-late protest. Not at the assignment to protect Sam, but at Lance's leaving.

The nurses' station was empty. The hallway was also vacant. He couldn't see the smoke yet from his vantage point, but that didn't mean it wasn't there. The floor had been evacuated and if the alarm hadn't been blaring, he knew the silence would have been eerie for a hospital floor. Fortunately, Sam's room was right next to the stairs. Clay could have him out of the room and off the floor within seconds if he needed to. The question was: Which was safer? Staying put or moving out into the open? Unsure of the answer, Lance decided to let Clay make that call. He trusted him to make the right one and knew Amber would, too.

Lance moved down the hall, trying to figure out how best to find her. He had to admit he was worried. The fact that she hadn't come back to Sam's room by now sent his brain envisioning all kinds of bad scenarios. Lance texted Trent. Where's Amber?

While waiting for Trent's reply, Lance decided to

head toward surgery and bolted for the stairs. If the man who'd demanded to see Amber had already been taken to surgery, the team would still be there working on him. They'd only evacuate if absolutely necessary. If the fire—or smoke—could be contained, parts of the hospital would be business as usual.

And so far Lance hadn't seen any indication of smoke or fire. He threw open the stairwell door and joined the crowd going down. His gaze scanned the faces as he flashed his badge and excused himself. While several looked familiar, none was the one he was looking for. His phone buzzed and he looked at the screen. A text from Trent. Amber left a little while ago with Tiffany. I escorted the prisoner to the surgical ward and surgery is proceeding as planned. Standing guard outside the surgery suite.

Lance paused. She wasn't there. Now what?

"Lance!"

He focused in on the voice. Tiffany at the bottom of the second level on the landing. He hurried toward her. "Where's Amber?"

"I got caught helping someone who fell. Everyone thinks they have to get out of the hospital immediately when they don't. They only need to evacuate where the fire is. But everyone is panicking when they just need to follow orders and get to a safe—"

"Where's Amber, Tiff?" He hated to cut her off, but the dread in his midsection refused to dissipate.

Tiffany raised a brow. "She went on up and said she was going to get Sam."

"When was this?"

"Just a short time ago. Maybe ten minutes? The woman I stopped to help broke her arm in the rush down the stairs. I thought Amber was going to stop, but she kept going."

Lance's concern shot straight to fear. If Amber had continued on, he would have seen her. So where had she gone?

Amber's already tense muscles contracted as they drew closer to Sam's room. They'd admitted him under an assumed name so she wasn't sure how this guy could have someone watching his room, but she had to assume he was. She continued the walk toward the room. The floor was empty—and filled with smoke. "Firefighters will be here soon," she said.

"Won't matter. We'll be gone. Go to him."

"You already know where Sam is," she said.

"What do you mean?"

"You said you had someone watching his room." He hesitated. "So you don't have someone watching his room."

"It doesn't matter, just go." He gave her another hard shove and she stumbled.

When she caught her balance, she shot him a glare. "You know where he is because of the tracker."

He frowned. "What?"

"We know about the tracker Pirhadi had placed in his shoe—one of two pairs that he'll wear."

He scowled then shrugged. "Yes, he had a tracker in both pairs."

Her anger flared up another notch. "So what do you need me for? Why not just come up here and get him?"

"Like that would happen with all the security he has around him. But as long as I have you as a hostage, people will obey."

A hostage. No, that wasn't going to happen. She was counting on Lance and Clay to have Sam protected somehow, some way. "How did you recognize me?"

"I didn't at first, but I knew Taj was hit and they'd bring him here. I was watching the OR waiting room and when you and that deputy came in it was pretty easy to figure out who you were."

Amber grimaced. So much for her disguise. She should have gone alone. "You're not taking Sam," she said.

"We'll see." It worried her that he didn't sound concerned. "It's ironic," he said. "All this time, I've been looking for a way to make some easy money and you were right there under my nose. Imagine my surprise when I found out."

Confusion flickered. "What are you talking about?"

"You haven't figured out who I am, have you?"

"No."

"That's because Kat didn't like pictures—or introducing me to the people she worked with. But a little snooping goes a long way. I found a picture of you and her in her nightstand one night after she fell asleep on the couch. She'd even written your name on the back and where the picture was taken. I was curious as to who this person was. Someone so important to her that she actually kept a picture. Not on her phone, of course. She wouldn't carry the picture with her. Once I managed to infiltrate her files, it was easy to find you and your current assignment. And easy to get in touch with Pirhadi."

Shock flared. "Vincent," she breathed.

"Nice to meet you, Amber."

"You used her." She arrived at the room and paused.

"Not at first. I fell for her, but she chose her job over me."

"So you betrayed her."

"It seemed to be a good idea at the time. Pirhadi paid a lot for the information on you. He was not a happy man when he found out. Now open the door."

Amber reached for the door handle. Once she pressed down, the door would swing inward. The gun dug into her side. But at least she was in front of the weapon. She knew she could make sure the first bullet would hit her before he could take aim at anyone else in the room. Then Lance or Clay would take down the man behind her. She opened the door and stepped inside. Two more steps brought her into the room where she stopped. Vincent stayed right behind her.

The room was empty. The relief nearly buckled her knees. She'd hoped, she'd prayed, she'd counted on them being quick enough to move him.

Vincent screamed. A howl that burned a painful path into her brain. "I'll just track him again," he raged. "I'll just find him again."

"I doubt it," Amber said.

"What are you talking about? I've had no trouble keeping up with him up to this point. Nothing's changed, it's just taking me a little longer."

"Everything's changed." She pointed.

Sam's shoes sat neatly in the center of the bed.

FIFTEEN

Lance hit the bottom of the stairs. No Amber. Several firemen, though. They were now on scene and it was going to be harder to find Amber in the chaos. She wasn't here, so where? *Think, man, think.* She'd go to Sam's room. Bottom line, no matter where she'd been, she'd return to Sam's room. He'd been an idiot to leave.

Lance raced back up stopping near the middle of the first-floor stairs. A hint of pink caught his eye back at the bottom. He almost ignored it, but decided to check it out. He spun, berating himself for wasting precious minutes and went back down the few stairs he'd just climbed. He rounded the bottom rail and looked down.

Amber's phone with the pink cover. That's why he'd stopped. Somewhere in his subconscious he remembered her pink phone. He snatched it and looked down at the screen. His calls and several texts were on the screen. He pocketed the device and tried to reassure himself that just because she'd dropped her phone in her rush to get to Sam didn't mean something bad had happened to her. Didn't mean it hadn't either.

The stairwell was now empty, and he took the stairs two at a time to the fourth floor. He burst through the door and encountered a wall of smoke. He pulled his shirt up over his mouth and nose then turned right.

"Hey, what are you doing up here? You need to get out!"

Lance turned to see a fireman pointing at the door. He was fully decked out in his suit. He spoke from behind the mask that muffled his words. But Lance understood him. "I'm getting out. Just need to check on something first."

"All the rooms up here are empty. We've got a grease fire on our hands. Someone threw water on it and it's spreading fast. Unless we can get it under control, we're going to lose this area."

Water on a grease fire. Not smart. Lance flashed his badge. "I'm checking this room."

The fireman held up his hand. "You've got about three seconds. Hurry up."

Lance pushed the door open and walked inside. This was Sam's old room. The room Amber would return to because she wouldn't realize Clay had moved him. "Empty."

"Told you. Now go, please." The man motioned him out of the room and Lance headed back down the stairs. A grease fire was deliberate. Which meant it was set to cause a distraction. So, someone had come on the floor and set the fire. Then left? Or stayed to watch in order to discover which room Sam would exit?

"Hey," he called after the retreating firefighter. "Hey, wait a minute." He breathed in the smoke and coughed. He lifted the collar of his shirt one more time up over his nose and mouth.

The fireman turned. "What?"

"Did you see anyone on this hall around this room?"

"There was a man and a woman up here just a minute ago. I sent them to the stairs just like I'm sending you. Go!"

"Which stairwell did they use?"

The fireman paused. "The one on the other end of the building." He pointed.

Lance raced down the hall to the stairs the man had indicated and threw open the door. He took the stairs at a run, using the railing to help propel him down even faster. When he arrived at the bottom, he pushed through the door and found himself near one of the exits. The fire alarm had ceased its head-pounding noise and in this area of the hospital he found all to be operating normally.

The problem was, there was an exit to his right, but also an exit down the hall and into the main lobby of the hospital. But that area was crawling with law enforcement and fire officials.

He bolted for the nearest exit. Someone had Amber, of that he had no doubt at this point. The combination of details simply added up to that. *A man and a woman,* the fireman had said. Amber's cell phone in the stairwell, the fact that she'd slipped away from Tiffany. And she hadn't found a way to get in touch with him yet. Everything added up to Amber being in trouble. But he didn't think he was too far behind her.

Once in the parking lot, he shivered and felt the falling flakes hit his cheeks. A fresh blanket of snow covered the area. Right now, with the temperature hovering in the low forties, most of the ice had melted and the new snow covered the slush underneath. Lance jogged closer to the cars, his gaze scanning the area.

And his eyes fell on a black SUV that had the motor

running, exhaust billowing from its tailpipe. He walked toward it. A window rolled down.

"Lance! Run!"

A gunshot sounded and he ducked.

Vincent sat in the seat behind the driver with the window down and was aiming the gun at Lance. She was in the backseat next to him. Amber clasped her hands together and brought them up in a volleyball serve motion to catch her abductor in the back of his head. He howled and swung a fist around. It landed on the side of her ear. The explosion of pain made her gasp. Stars sparkled in front of her eyes and blackness swirled.

But she heard his weapon hit the side of the car. "Drive! Go!" he yelled and turned to glare at Amber. She raised her hands ready to defend herself should he decide to punch her again.

"Where's Yousef's son, Amber?" the man in the front demanded. He turned in the seat and she found herself staring at the business end of yet another weapon.

Amber let out another gasp when she realized who faced her. Deon Pirhadi, Yousef's brother and Sam's uncle. A man she'd seen a number of times over the past four years. "Sam's safe."

"Tell me where he is."

"I have no idea."

He growled and turned to put the car in gear. "Vincent? Where's Sam?"

She tried to catch his eyes in the mirror, but he was busy backing out of the parking place. Stupid. She would have backed in if she was going to kidnap someone and needed to make a fast getaway. The thought was fleeting, a desperate attempt to keep her cool. To reassure herself that her brain was still functioning and she could find a way to either outsmart them and escape or just plain get away.

"I couldn't get him," Vincent said. "Somehow they found out about the tracker in Sam's shoes and they moved him. But we've got her, and that means we're very close to getting him."

Amber sat in the backseat behind the open passenger seat. Vincent sat to her left. She strained to see Lance and saw him racing for the nearest officer. He would come after her. Somehow she had to make sure he could keep her in sight. Without getting him killed.

Deon handed the weapon to Vincent. "Try not to lose this one."

Vincent scowled and fear drew Amber's shoulder muscles tighter and flexed them while she pushed the fear away. They wouldn't kill her. Not yet. Not as long as they thought she could lead them to Sam. Somehow she was going to work that to her advantage. She just had to think of a way to do so. And she truthfully had no idea where Sam was, so in a way, that was a blessing. Clay would protect the child with his life. There was no more tracker, no way to find him now. She could be thankful for that anyway. "You're too late," she said.

"What?"

"Sam already told us everything." If they knew Sam had shared the information he'd gotten from his father's office, they'd have no reason to kill him, right?

Vincent chuckled. "Not likely."

"Not likely that he told us about Ravi?"

Deon swore as he peeled out of the hospital parking lot. "That cop is behind us. You should have shot him when you had the chance. You are a lousy marksman. Not enough visits to the shooting range, eh?"

Vincent went rigid. His fury made his hand shake, and Amber sincerely wished he would remove his finger from the trigger. "Better not pull that trigger," she said softly. "I'm guessing you don't have all of your money yet."

He blinked at her and drew in a deep breath through his nose. And while he didn't move his finger, he did aim the gun slightly over her shoulder, which afforded her a little breathing room. But his eyes didn't leave hers and Deon kept flicking glances at her in the rearview mirror. "What do you know about Ravi?" Deon asked.

"That he's on a plane bringing you a virus."

The car jerked, and he let out a string of curse words that told her she'd hit her mark. "Yes," he snarled. "A virus that is going to make me very, very rich and will bring America's banking system to her knees."

Amber stilled. "What? A computer virus?"

"A very powerful computer virus."

So not a virus that would kill people. Relief swept her. Then she tensed again. He still had to be stopped, and Sam had to be rescued.

She glanced at the door. Locked. She wondered if the child locks were on.

"Give me your hands."

"What?" She looked at Vincent.

He held the gun in one hand and a roll of duct tape in another. "Give me your hands!"

"No." If she let him tie her hands up, that would be it. He couldn't hold the gun on her and tape her up at the same time. The car swerved to the left and rounded the corner. She slammed into the door and pain shot through her right shoulder as the big SUV's tires caught a patch of ice and slid. She ignored the pain and took advantage of the moment to unlock the door.

"What are you doing, Deon?" Vincent yelled. "You're not driving on a dry highway, man."

"I've got to lose that cop and warn Yousef that the meeting is compromised."

"You're going to lose everything if you kill us."

"You have a better idea? You? Who couldn't even grab a little boy and return him to his father? Incompetent imbecile," he muttered. Amber's gaze shot to the road. Deon had managed to keep the vehicle on the street and right now it was a straight shot to the highway. At least he'd come prepared and had chains on the tires, but even chains wouldn't do him much good on ice. The road they were now on had been scraped and Deon would find it much easier to drive on it. Easier and faster. She tried to picture the route in her mind. They'd leave the city area, hit a short patch of wooded back road and come out the highway exit ramp.

She turned and looked out the back window. Lance was nowhere to be seen. Her heart thudded. But Deon didn't go straight, he pulled into a side alley and turned a gun on her face. How many weapons did he have up there? A full arsenal no doubt. "Now," Deon said, "give him your hands or I put a bullet in you."

"Then how will you get Sam?"

He smirked. "I have a feeling I'm not going to be able to get him through you anyway. You would die for that loser."

Amber lunged at him and only Vincent's hard shove kept her from punching the man in the mouth. And probably saved her from getting shot. She landed hard against the door once more. Her shoulder protested the harsh treatment. She drew in a ragged breath and stared at Deon. "You and Yousef don't deserve to breathe the same air as Sam," she whispered.

Deon's eyes, so like his brother's, glittered. "Tape her up before I simply decide to shoot her. And put some tape over her mouth."

Vincent set his gun down and grabbed her hands. She clenched her jaw and let him duct tape them together doing her best to keep her wrists separated without him noticing. He wrapped the tape several times. Tight. She winced and flexed her fingers when he ripped the roll from the piece now restricting her. Then glanced behind them one more time.

Still no Lance.

"I need a vehicle, Clay. Preferably one that won't blow a tire!" It had probably been the bullet that damaged the tire enough for it to give out during the chase.

"I've got Ronnie bringing you one now."

"And get someone on the highway exit." Lance paced in front of his SUV. The tire had blown and he'd ridden on it as far as he could, trying to keep up with Amber and her abductors. Then he'd had no choice but to stop. His heart beat a heavy rhythm in his chest and prayers flew from his lips. "I'm thinking he'll want to get Amber out of town and far away as fast as possible. He may even head to the airport."

"Then he'll make his demands especially if we manage to get our hands on whatever it is Ravi is bringing him. He'll want to use Amber as a bargaining chip. I'll request flights to be grounded and get his picture distributed to airport security."

"I agree. When does the plane land?"

"In three hours."

Ronnie pulled up beside him. Lance climbed into the passenger seat and pointed. "Follow those tracks for now. As soon as he hits the highway, we won't know which way to go."

Ronnie did as asked and Lance sat on the edge of the seat. He didn't bother with a seat belt. As soon as he found Amber, he wanted to be out of the vehicle. *Please, dear God, don't let anything happen to her. Lead me to her. Keep her safe.*

He believed God heard his prayer. Believed it with everything in him. But he also knew that God didn't just make everything okay because He was asked. Amber's kidnapping hadn't taken Him by surprise. He knew it was coming. He could have stopped it. But He hadn't. Lance wanted to know why, but couldn't think about that right now. He just wanted to find her and keep her safe. Forever. "If that's all right with You, God," he whispered.

"What?" Ronnie asked.

"Nothing," Lance murmured. "You see anything?"

"No, nothing."

"Head for the highway."

SIXTEEN

Amber had to get out of the car. She was going to have to take a chance and do something. But what? Her fingers were starting to go numb. She wiggled them to keep the blood flowing.

A curse reached her. Deon swerved down a side road and Amber clutched the handle on the door with her bound hands to keep from slamming into Vincent. When the car steadied, she sucked in a breath and looked up to find Vincent glaring out the back window. She turned to see what had him so angry then breathed a prayer of thanks when she realized Lance had caught back up with them. Their brief stop to tape her hands had bought her the much-needed time Lance needed to find her. He was quite a ways back, but at least he was there. And he wasn't trying to be subtle, he had the lights flashing and the siren going.

And thanks to Deon's wild driving, Vincent's weapon was no longer aimed at her. Amber grabbed the door handle once again, shifted in the seat for leverage and drew her foot back. She kicked out, catching Vincent in the head. He cried out and his weapon fell to the floorboard. Amber lunged for it and felt something slam into the back of her head.

She gasped at the pain even as her fingers closed over the barrel of the gun. Deon was yelling something then the car jerked and she lost her grip. Her spine rammed into the back of the front seat, the weapon slid away and Amber wanted to scream her frustration. She fell to the floor between the backseat and the front, her head spinning. Vincent had retrieved the weapon and was hanging out the open window aiming the gun at the approaching police vehicle.

Cold air rushed over her, clearing her head a bit. A gunshot made her flinch and her ears ring. She lifted her gaze and reached up with her bound hands to press the unlock button. Vincent was too busy taking aim for his shot to pay her attention.

Heart pounding, head throbbing, she swallowed a wave of nausea and reached for the door handle. She had to avoid Vincent's legs and work around his body to reach it, but she managed. Her fingers, clumsy and almost numb, finally closed around the handle. The car swerved again, but Amber clenched her teeth and yanked.

The door opened and with Vincent's weight almost fully on it to give him leverage, the door swung open. Vincent, caught halfway out of the window, scrambled to hold on and get back in the vehicle. Amber moved as quickly as she could from her awkward position on the floor and got to her knees, slid her taped hands under Vincent's knees and hefted the man out the door.

His scream echoed around her as he tumbled from the vehicle. "You—" She closed her ears to the names he called her. He held on to the window frame. "Stop the car, stop the car!" His screams fueled her determination.

Amber slammed her hands down on his fingers. Vincent gave another harsh cry and let go. He disappeared from view. Deon kept going, his curses ringing in her ears. The back door slammed shut and Amber now had a new problem. She had to get the car stopped, but knew there was no way Deon was going to stop and try to pick up his partner in crime as long as there was a police vehicle behind him. Amber climbed into the backseat and looked over her shoulder. No Lance. He'd fallen back when Vincent had started shooting at him.

Deon glared at her in the rearview mirror. "You're going to pay for this."

"We'll see." Amber curled her fingers into fists, brought her hands up then down like a sledgehammer on Deon's ear.

He cried out and slammed on the brakes. The big SUV tried to stop, but couldn't find traction on the snow and ice. The vehicle spun. Amber dropped back onto the floor, her breath coming in gasps. She looked for Vincent's gun, but realized it must have gone out the door with him.

The vehicle spun again and the impact jerked her against the back of Deon's seat. She heard the screeching crunch of metal and Deon's cry. Then stillness. Amber groaned, stunned at the sudden jolt, but didn't think she was hurt. The car had hit—and rolled up—a hill, its front passenger side tire wedged beneath a large fallen tree trunk. Thankfully, as she was on the floorboard, her position cushioned her against the full effects of the crash. The fact that the SUV was built like a tank and Deon had taken his foot off the gas when she'd shoved Vincent out the door helped, as well. Only now she had to move. She tried to see Deon's head, but was too low.

Where was Lance? Was he still back there?

With her hands still taped together, she reached for the door. She got her fingers hooked around the handle and pulled. It opened again and Amber stumbled into the snow expecting to feel the impact of a bullet at any moment.

Nausea blindsided her and she wondered if she had a concussion. She rose to her feet, knees shaking, adrenaline rushing. She shot a quick glance around and didn't see Vincent. She leaned against the SUV and lifted her knee up. Then she brought her hands down hard while pulling to separate her wrists.

The tape ripped and her hands were finally free. Sharp pains shot through her fingers as the blood flowed once again. Amber quickly removed the excess tape and tossed it to the ground. She moved fast, worried Deon would get to a weapon before she had the chance to get to one first. She glanced at the front seat and saw him leaning against the steering wheel, eyes closed. Was he truly hurt, or was he faking it as she had done when Lance had found her?

She could hear the sirens approaching. The Wrangler's Corner police vehicle pulled to a stop about twenty yards away. She had backup. Lance climbed out of the vehicle and started to head her way. "Look for the guy who fell out of the car!" She glanced around again, looking for the man. She'd shoved him out maybe half a mile back. "Did you see him fall out?"

"No, what happened?"

"I pushed him out."

"Didn't see him." Lance turned to the officer behind him. "Why don't you see if you can find him? We can take care of this and more backup's on the way."

"Got it." Ronnie nodded and jogged through the snow back toward the vehicle. He hopped in and did a three-point turn to head back in the direction they'd come from.

Amber moved toward the driver's door and peered at the man behind the wheel. Still Deon hadn't moved. "Deon Pirhadi! Come out of the vehicle with your hands up." He didn't respond to her call.

A shot rang out. The bullet slammed the ground beside her and she dropped to her knees and rolled under the SUV.

Lance heard the gunshot and saw Amber drop and disappear under the belly of the SUV that now lay crunched up against the tree. Lance raced toward the wrecked vehicle as it offered the nearest protection against further gunshots. He ducked behind it and another shot sounded. He flinched, but noticed it didn't come near him. He lay flat on the ground, but the way the car was tilted up against the hill and the tree, he couldn't roll under it to join Amber, but he could see her. She lay on her belly, her eyes trained in the direction the shot had come from. "Amber!"

She turned to look at him. "Stay down, Lance, it's probably Vincent shooting."

"Ronnie went after him."

"Don't think he's got him yet," she grunted. "I hope you have a gun on you."

"Yes, of course."

"Good, can you see if the driver is still unconscious?"

Lance rose high enough to look in the window. He could see the man slumped over the wheel. "He's not moving." He tried the door, but it wouldn't open. He hadn't thought it would, but had to try. He pulled on the back door, and to his surprise, it opened. He started to crawl into the backseat but felt the car shift. The driver still didn't move.

Another crack sounded and the bullet pinged off the vehicle. Lance ducked back out and dropped to the ground to see that Amber had rolled even farther under the belly of the car. "I can't get in. The car's not stable enough. I'm afraid it will shift and crush you."

"And there's only one way out from under here."

He understood what she meant. If she rolled out, the sniper could pick her off. "Just stay put for the moment."

"Fine, but he's got a gun in there. We'll have to be careful," she breathed. "Where's backup?"

"Should be here soon. The roads are still pretty bad. They'll have to go slower than usual."

Amber nodded.

Lance scanned the area. He couldn't figure out where the shooter was, he just had the man's general direction. The car swayed.

"Lance, check on Deon again, will you? I don't need him getting out of the car and the thing coming down on me."

"Deon's the driver?"

"Yes, Sam's uncle."

Lance maneuvered himself beside the vehicle and looked in again. Deon was moving.

And so was the car.

The shooting had stopped for the moment. He heard

sirens and finally heard the chopper coming from above. Police vehicles rolled into the area.

The car shuddered again.

"Amber, you're going to have to chance it and roll out. Tiffany and the others are here. They'll cover you." He looked in the front seat again. Deon leaned back against the seat, clutching his head. The SUV shifted. "Amber, get out!"

Amber rolled, scrambled to her feet and raced around the back of the vehicle to Lance's side. No shot came their way. Lance held his weapon trained on the man behind the wheel. Deon looked up. Blood ran from a nasty cut above his right eye. Lance saw the moment comprehension returned.

He blinked. Then swiped the blood and narrowed his eyes.

Amber slipped away from him and he watched her duck down next to the driver's door. Lance kept his gaze locked on the man who'd helped kidnap Amber and tried to kill her and Sam. Part of him wanted Deon to do something stupid, to justify Lance in pulling the trigger. But the other part, the bigger part of himself, told him to keep it together and follow the law. "Don't move, Deon."

The man's jaw tightened and his eyes flickered. Then his door opened and he disappeared from view. Lance raced around to the other side of the car to find Amber sitting on top of the man, arm cocked back and fingers balled into a hard fist. "Move and I'll add to your concussion." She didn't glance away from her prisoner. "Lance, would you please get his gun from the floorboard?" The politely phrased question didn't hide the steel in her voice—or the tightly leashed rage he could see on her face.

"Ronnie," he spoke into his radio, "I need an update."

"Shooter is in custody."

Relief flowed. "Thanks."

"But I've got bad news."

"What's that?"

"Clay was ambushed coming out of the hospital. Sam's gone."

SEVENTEEN

Amber's heart dropped. Fear exploded through her. "Gone?" She stared at Lance then turned her gaze on Ronnie who'd just driven up. She'd seen him and Lance in a heated discussion while she spoke with one of the other deputies who'd arrived. When she'd intercepted Lance's frantic gaze, she'd hurried over. Only to hear Sam had been taken. "Gone?" Ronnie took a step back and she didn't care if she was scaring the man. "How is he just gone?" she yelled. "How is that even possible? Clay had him. He wouldn't let anything happen to him."

"Clay's shot," Lance said. "They got him getting into his car."

She gasped, her fury fizzling with the news and her fear skyrocketing. "Shot? How bad? He's not—" She couldn't say the word, but Lance was already shaking his head.

"No, he's not dead. Someone saw it happen and called it in. He's being taken care of at the hospital in Nashville and we've got a chopper in the air looking for Sam."

"Did you get a vehicle description?" Amber asked.

"Yes, got it on camera in fact," Ronnie said. He cleared his throat. "It was a white Rolls-Royce."

Amber nearly choked on her next breath. "That's Sam's father's car. He never drives anything else. If he didn't drive it out here, he rented it."

"There was mass confusion in the hospital," Ronnie said, "especially on the lower floors, people were everywhere and some were panicking in spite of the staff reassuring them. There was also a bomb threat called in so there was an evacuation going on, as well. So, Clay called me, said y'all were at the hospital and that to play it safe, he was going to have to move Sam. Said he was taking him to the Starke ranch and to let you know where they were. Then I got the call about the shooting. Trent's with Clay now and sending me updates. Sabrina's on her way with a police escort."

Amber rubbed her eyes and her heart shuddered with her fear. Fear for her brother, fear for Sam. And anger. Lots and lots of anger. "It's a computer virus, Lance. They're planning to hack into the banking system."

"So not a virus that could wipe out people?"

"No. So honestly my first priority is to find Sam." She began to pace. She had to think it through. "This was an incredibly risky move on Yousef's part. Incredibly risky. Why would he do it? He could have waited until Sam was out of the hospital, but he didn't. Why?"

"He's on a time deadline," Lance said.

She looked at him. "The plane. It's got to have something to do with when the plane lands."

"You were the distraction," Lance said softly. "All of this was just a distraction. Pirhadi had every intention of getting to Sam himself. He sent his brother and other killers after you here at the hospital, but he got Sam himself—his real target."

"Yes," she whispered. "Of course. He changed the meeting place, managed to get Ravi and his partner on another flight and now is planning to close the deal."

"Sam is his insurance. If law enforcement catches up to him, he has a bargaining tool. No one is going to do anything to get a child killed. They might not be so careful with you as a hostage, but—"

She nodded. "You're right." She glanced at him. "How much longer until the plane lands?"

"Less than an hour. Law enforcement is set up and ready to act."

"Pirhadi will take Sam to the meeting place. If the men don't meet him, he'll know something is wrong."

Lance frowned. "Law enforcement is waiting for the plane to land. They'll let the people get off the plane one by one and simply pull our two suspects aside the minute they set foot into the gate area. Whatever they're supposed to deliver will be carried on the plane with them, I'm sure."

Amber closed her eyes. A headache was beating at her temples like it was trying to burst forth. "All right, we'll need to find out the meeting place.

"Which is why we need to follow those men instead of detaining them." She clasped his hand. "We have no choice, Lance. If Pirhadi is tipped off that we know what's going on and we know who he's meeting, he'll disappear." And she'd lose Sam forever. The crushing thought nearly took her to her knees. But she had to be strong.

Lance blew out a breath. "I don't know if we can stop it now."

"We have to. For Sam. Do you know who Clay's contact was?"

"Yes. His name's Owen Jones. He's the lead special agent on this one."

"Then let him know what's going on. And we have to make sure that Deon doesn't have a chance to contact his brother. He knows that Sam told us everything and that we've figured it out. Most of it anyway. If he tells Yousef…"

Lance pulled his phone from his pocket and then handed her the one that belonged to her. "Found it in the stairwell," he said.

"Thanks. Let's get to the airport. You can make the calls on the way. I'll drive." Amber prayed for Sam, for Clay, for everyone involved in this drama that seemed to have no end. *Please, God, let this all have a happy ending.*

Lance hung up on his fourth call. He'd gotten Deon Pirhadi in isolation. No calls coming in or going out. He'd been transported to one of the Nashville hospitals since the Wrangler's Corner one was still in chaos. Vincent was also under heavy guard at the same hospital having sustained a concussion thanks to his tumble from the vehicle. Which was probably why his aim was so bad when he was shooting at them after the crash— and why it was so easy to apprehend him. Ronnie said he'd had no trouble finding the man. He'd managed to walk close enough to see the wreck, fired a couple of shots then passed out.

Now for the hard part. He dialed Owen's number. The man answered, surprising Lance. "Jones here."

"Yes, Special Agent Jones, this is Deputy Lance Goode. I'm calling for Clay Starke."

"Why isn't Clay calling me?"

"He's been shot."

Silence came across the line. Then, he responded, "I see. Is he going to make it?"

"Yes, he is, but that's not why I'm calling. I need you to stand down on the two men coming in on the flight from Atlanta."

"Want to tell me why?"

"It's a long story."

"You've got five minutes."

Lance summarized the situation as best he could with frequent glances at Amber. Her nods of approval spurred him on. "It's a computer virus, not a disease. That's why we need to let them get out of the airport. We have to follow them in order to apprehend the ringleader."

"You're sure about this?"

"Absolutely one hundred percent positive."

"Meet me here in the cell phone parking lot."

"I'm on the way. We're in a Ford Interceptor with chains on the tires."

Lance disconnected the call and told Amber where to go. Her white knuckles on the steering wheel and her pinched face were a good indication of her worry. "He's going to be okay. This is going to work."

"If they agree. It's a huge risk to let them leave the airport."

He shook his head. "I don't know. It might be safer for everyone if they're not in a place where something could go wrong and they could snatch hostages."

They both fell silent and Lance watched her drive.

She'd hit the highway and they'd both been relieved to find it had been scraped. She went exactly the speed limit. There was no need to hurry as they'd arrive to the airport before the plane landed. He stayed quiet and let his thoughts go to places he'd refused to go to before.

To Amber.

A beautiful, amazing woman who'd lived a life of danger, secrecy and sacrifice. Truly, it was hard for him to wrap his mind around it, but he was living this with her so staying in denial wasn't an option. And Sam...the quirky little boy had captured his heart. *Please, God, let us find him, please don't let anything happen to him.*

Amber. Sam. Two people he'd grown to care about. One he'd known his entire life. The other, a short time. Two people he didn't want to say goodbye to.

But he'd sworn never to marry again. Never to allow himself to be in a place where he could be hurt that way again. Was he a coward? Or just so scarred he'd never be able to get to the point where he could trust a woman enough to marry her? Then again, was it really fair to compare Amber to his deceased wife? Then again, how did one marry and build a life with a CIA operative? And why was he even thinking along those lines? Because he cared. He loved her. She'd wound her way into his heart. Her kindness after Krissy died, the light touches, the sweet smiles whenever she was around him. And now being with her 24/7 over the last few days. He knew he could play the denial game, but he loved her. *Oh God, You sent her and Sam to me, didn't You?* He knew people had been praying for him to open his heart to someone else. He gave a mental snort. He was quite sure Amber hadn't been the one they'd prayed for him to be with, though.

He turned away with a slight shake of his head and watched the airport come into view. Amber made her way to the cell phone lot and backed into the nearest spot.

A large gray van sat about ten yards to their right. The door opened and a large man dressed in plain clothes stepped out and walked their way. Lance got out of the car and held out a hand. The special agent shook it and then did the same with Amber. "I've discussed this situation with the team. Now that we know the virus is the work of hackers and not going to kill people, we've come to the agreement that we'll allow the two men to leave the airport and follow them to the meeting place. Not just for the boy's sake, but because we want Pirhadi. We've had our eye on him for a while now. We've just never been able to catch him."

"Join the club," Amber muttered.

Lance nodded.

"The plane is actually a little early. We'll let you know when we have Pirhadi in custody."

"I'm going with you," Amber said.

"No, ma'am, you're not."

"Yes, sir, I am." Lance heard the steel in her voice and knew she'd win. "Sam trusts me, he'll listen to me. Unless you're skilled at dealing with autistic six-year-olds, I suggest you let me do it."

The man hesitated. "Are you law enforcement?"

"Yes."

"What branch?"

"I don't share that."

Special Agent Jones's brows rose. "Huh. Any ID on you?"

"No."

He looked at Lance. "CIA?"

Lance shrugged.

Jones rolled his eyes. "All right. You can follow. Stay with the van. I need a number to call."

She gave him Kat's number. He made the call, listened for a brief moment then hung up. "Guess you're in."

"Could you provide us with an earpiece?" Amber asked.

Another hesitation then he nodded. "Hold on a second." When he returned, he had the requested items. Lance and Amber inserted the small devices in their ears, climbed into their vehicle and waited for the signal that the mission was under way.

Amber breathed prayers for Sam's safety as they fell in behind the gray van. Kat hadn't deserted them or betrayed her. She'd been handling things from behind the scenes like she was supposed to do.

A chopper hovered above, but disappeared. She knew it would follow at a discreet distance so as not to tip off the men they were made. *God, I really don't understand why this is happening, but I guess I have a choice. I can believe that You're in control and this didn't take You by surprise. Please keep Sam safe.* Bad stuff happened because people made bad decisions that had consequences that affected others. God wasn't mad at her, God wasn't punishing her for something. This situation was the result of Pirhadi's decisions and Sam was in danger because of those decisions.

And God could use Amber to do something about Pirhadi. Her fingers flexed on the wheel. "Where are we going, Jones?" she asked.

"They had a rental car reservation. We had an agent at the counter and she passed on which car they'd be in. We've got a tracker and a listening device on the car. They're heading for an old farmhouse off Route 2. ETA is ten minutes."

"Did they say anything about Sam?"

"No."

Amber drew in a deep breath. This was it. If they could catch Pirhadi in this deal then it would be over. Everything. And Nadia wouldn't have died in vain. Her final goal in life would have been achieved. Her husband would no longer be a danger to her son or anyone else.

Soon, they were slowing. The van pulled into a copse of trees and disappeared. She followed it. "I know this area," Lance said. "The farmhouse is about half a mile up ahead."

"Yes, I know this place, too. Heather Frank used to live out here." Excitement curled through her. "There's a tree house in the back. A sniper would have a good view of the house from up there."

"This may really work to our advantage for us because it's surrounded by trees. They'll never see us coming."

"Us?"

"Well, the feds, I guess."

"And me." She opened the door. "I'm going to get Sam."

Lance got out, as well. "Amber, I don't think that's a good idea."

She turned to him and took a deep breath. "Lance, I have to do this. I couldn't save his mother, but I can help save him. He trusts me."

Lance nodded and shoved his hands in his pockets.

Amber glanced around. Law enforcement was moving. Swarming, actually. She made her way over to Special Agent Jones. "Let me go in, please."

"Ma'am—"

"It's Amber. I'm trained for this. And I need to see where Sam is. If he's loose, not tied up somewhere, I can get him out and you can raid the place, shoot it up or burn it down, I don't care. Just let me see if I can get to Sam."

His eyes bored holes in hers. "I spoke with your handler, but I'm still not sure…"

She sighed. "I've been undercover as Sam's nanny for the past four years. The short version is that my handler's ex-boyfriend turned traitor and sold me out to Pirhadi. She wants to stop him almost as much as I do. Let me finish this assignment."

"I see," he said. "All right. I was listening to your conversation in the car. You know this place?"

"I do."

"It was for lease," the agent said. "Someone rented it two days ago and signed the lease for three months but from the information we've managed to gather in the short amount of time that we learned of the place, no one's been living there."

"They leased it for this reason," Amber said. "This day."

"Yes, that's what it looks like."

"It's a small house with two bedrooms and one bathroom at the back. The main part of the house is open concept. There's a kitchen to the right that opens up into one large living area in the middle with a bar kind of separating the two rooms." She pointed. "There's the front door that you can see from here and another to the side of the house that leads into the kitchen. Around the back, there are sliding glass doors that lead from the deck into the house."

"All right. We'll have you covered as you approach. My agents will be right behind you, looking for a good hiding place." He handed her a Kevlar vest and she slipped it on. Then he gave her a pair of glasses. "Use these. They have a camera and a mic on them so we'll be able to see what you see and hear what you hear. Keep the earpiece so you can hear us."

She slipped them on her nose. She was ready. She shivered in the afternoon air. The temperatures had risen, but it was still chilly. Midfifties and the snow was melting. At least she wouldn't have to try to navigate over ice. There might be patches in the shade, but she'd be careful and would be able to approach the house along the tree line without being seen. She hoped.

She found Lance watching her. She walked over to him and he wrapped her in a hug and kissed the top of her head. "Be careful," he whispered in her ear.

"I will, I promise."

"You can sit in the van and watch," Jones told Lance.

He nodded then kissed her. Amber let him, relishing the feel of his mouth on hers. She kissed him back trying to convey what was in her heart. He released her and she swallowed hard. "We'll talk later."

Lance nodded. "I'll be here when you bring Sam out."

"Good. I want you here."

Then she spun on her heel and took off for the house, her booted feet leaving a trail behind on the slushy ground. The closer she got, the faster her heart beat.

When the house came into view, she stopped and drew in a calming breath. She could do this. She *would* do this. Sam was counting on her and she wouldn't let him down. Amber looked at the front yard. The snow covered the ground and she saw no footprints in the yard, but she could see the ones leading from the car to the front door. The white Rolls blended with the background. The dark rental sedan had pulled next to it in the drive. Amber darted for the side of the home to the nearest window.

EIGHTEEN

Lance watched the screen and saw Amber at the window. She looked in and he saw what she saw. An empty bedroom. She withdrew and walked around the side of the house to the next window. Blinds prevented her from seeing in. She tried to push the window up, but he assumed it was locked since she turned away.

The image on the monitor stilled and for a moment he wondered if the feed had frozen. Then he realized that she'd paused and was thinking about her next move. Finally, she shifted again and walked to the front door. His heart pounded and he wanted to scream at her to get away. Instead, he saw her hand reach for the doorknob. She turned it and he saw that it wasn't locked. She let go and stepped back then walked off the porch to go around the opposite side of the house. He felt like he was walking beside her. She was now at the back porch, a wooden deck. She walked up the steps to the sliding glass doors and stood to the side.

On another monitor, Lance saw two agents maneuver into the trees behind her. He figured one would be in the tree house. Within seconds the house was surrounded.

No one was coming out of there and leaving. But no one would see a soul if he looked out of the window.

Screams erupted from the house. "Game! Game! Game!"

"Shut the kid up!"

He heard a shuffle then Amber's indrawn breath.

Sam continued to howl his rage.

And then another monitor lit up. They had eyes in the house. He could see the kitchen and into the living area. Amber had found a window and managed to slip a tiny camera in next to the windowpane.

And Lance got his first view of the three men who'd caused him and Amber and Sam so much grief. He recognized Yousef from his picture. The man held Sam's arm in a tight grip while the boy cried and yelled.

The other two men looked impatient and disgusted with the entire episode. Pirhadi lifted his weapon and placed it against Sam's head. To Lance's horror, he could see the man had every intention of killing his son where he stood.

And then Amber stepped into the room.

Lance gasped.

The agent behind him did the same.

She'd run from the back to the front door and walked inside. "Stop!" She held a hand up. "Don't hurt him!" The other two men in the room lifted their weapons and trained them on her. "Let him come to me," she said, her focus on Pirhadi. "Let him go." Sam stopped mid-wail and looked at her. His chest heaved his indignation.

Lance couldn't breathe. She was going to get killed. She wore a vest, but that wouldn't stop a head shot.

"What are you doing here?" Pirhadi raged. He paced, dragging Sam with him.

"I came to get Sam," Amber said. She walked toward them.

One of the other men went to the window and looked out to the front where the vehicles were. When he turned, his face held an ugly scowl. "Stay where you are." Amber stopped. "How did you get here? There is no car."

"I walked."

"From where?"

"From where I left my car," she said. "I didn't want you to know I was here. Now give me Sam."

Pirhadi transferred his weapon from Sam's head to aim it at Amber's heart. "You are a very foolish woman, Amber Starke."

"And you are a very evil man." She lifted her chin. "But you're surrounded by the FBI and other law enforcement and you won't be leaving here." She lowered her head and Lance saw the briefcase on the floor next to the man who hadn't moved or spoken yet. The virus the man in the hospital had mentioned?

"Game, Number One Mom, please," Sam said. His small voice caused her heart to ache. She wanted to gather him to her and protect him, to make him forget the things he was now experiencing.

She held out a hand. "Come here, Sam."

"Game." He looked at the floor. "Game now, please."

"Sam—"

"Ravi," he said. The man to her right jerked. "Seven, six, two, five. Plane. Ravi has a virus."

Pirhadi looked at his son, his fury mounting. "You stupid boy."

Amber ignored the urge to grab the gun from where

it nestled against her back and shoot the man herself. She looked at Sam. "Sam, stop. We'll play chess in a little while. Come to me."

Sam took a step toward her and Pirhadi yanked him back. Sam cried out his anger at the harsh treatment.

"Shut up," Pirhadi snarled. "Both of you!" This time he ignored Sam's loud cries and motioned with his weapon to the briefcase. "Paulo, let's get this done and then I'll dispose of these two."

"What about the law enforcement she said was out there?" Paulo asked.

"There's no one out there," he sneered. "She's CIA. They work alone. They go undercover, and they infiltrate your house to steal your trust." He spat in her direction. "And they turn your wife against you."

"She was already turned before I got there," Amber said softly.

"Why does the kid say my name? What does he know about the virus?" This quiet question came from the man to her right. The one with the briefcase. Ravi, Amber deduced. Sam had stilled, his cries quieted, but she heard his sniffles and they nearly broke her heart.

"It doesn't matter," Pirhadi all but shouted. "Let's get this done."

Sam flinched and cringed then screamed. "Game!"

His father shoved him aside and Sam fell to the floor near the kitchen bar area. Amber raced to his side, ignoring the guns that followed her. She gathered Sam to her, and he clutched her while she glared at Pirhadi. "That wasn't necessary," Amber said as Sam cried against her shoulder.

Pirhadi's face went bloodred. He screamed and fired

a shot at the ceiling and then turned the weapon on her and Sam.

"Now," she whispered, knowing the agents were listening, waiting for her to signal. "Now." She rolled with Sam into the kitchen and pulled him behind the counter.

The front door burst in. "Federal agents! Freeze! Drop your weapons! Drop them now!"

A series of pops sounded and she hovered over Sam who struggled against her. "Be still, Sam, please. Just be still." And he stopped his struggles and let her keep him against her.

When the shooting stopped, Amber pulled away from Sam who never looked at her, but scooted until his back was against the wall of the bar.

Amber pulled the glasses from her face, set them on the floor and removed her weapon. She peered around the edge of the bar. Pirhadi was on the floor, blood spilling from his chest. The other two men, Paulo and Ravi, had their hands above their heads. She turned back to Sam and pulled him back into her lap. Surprised that he didn't protest, she waited, keeping him safe while the agents took care of the men who'd tried to kill them. Once it was clear that she and Sam were fine law enforcement left them alone. The minutes ticked by. The chaos continued.

"Amber!"

Lance. She drew in a deep breath and looked up. He stood over her. His dear face was drawn with worry, his eyes roved over her and Sam seeming to take in every detail. Relief then filled his features and he reached to touch her cheek. "They wouldn't let me in any sooner."

"It's okay," she whispered. "It's over, it's really over."

He dropped his hand. "Pirhadi's dead."

"Yes. I thought so."

He dropped beside her and Sam and took her hand. "You saved his life again."

She looked at him and then at Sam who lay against her, his eyes shut. He felt warm, like he might still have a low-grade fever. "Did you see Yousef's face when he turned his gun on him?" she asked softly.

"I was watching on the monitor. I saw it." He blinked and looked away for a moment and she thought she saw tears there. When he looked back they were gone. "I saw it and I could do nothing." He squeezed her fingers. "You did the only thing you could do. You had no choice."

"I didn't even stop to think about the consequences. I just acted."

"And you saved him. Pirhadi can't hurt anyone ever again."

Sam opened his eyes. "Number One Dad is dead."

"Yes," Amber said and stroked his hair.

Sam sat up. "Number One Mom is dead."

Amber felt tears choke her. "Yes, Sam, I'm sorry."

Sam touched her cheek. "Amber. Number One Mom now. Number One Mom keep Sam safe. No more bad guys. No more scared."

She stared at him in wonder. He understood. In his own way, he was processing everything, but he understood. "That's right, Sam, you don't have to be afraid anymore."

"No more."

She touched his forehead. "Come on, Sam, let's get you…" *where?* "somewhere…and get you well."

"Get well," Sam echoed.

"Yes."

Lance stood and picked Sam up then held out a hand to Amber. "Come on, let's go home."

Amber stared at him. Where was home?

He must have understood her confusion because he gave her a small smile. "Christmas is tomorrow. Your mother is expecting you."

She raised a brow. "All right then. Home it is."

Christmas Day dawned sunny and bright. Her stomach rumbled at the smell of bacon, eggs, toast and cinnamon rolls. She'd missed her mother's cooking.

Amber rolled from the bed she'd crashed into in the wee hours of the morning. Lance had dropped her and Sam off at her parents' ranch, kissed her goodbye and left. She'd wanted to beg him to stay, but had kept her lips shut. Mostly because she had some decisions to make. Truly, in her heart, she'd already made them. She'd texted Kat last night and told her they needed to talk. Kat had texted back that she thought that talk might be coming, but to have a merry Christmas and she'd be in touch soon.

Amber looked at the other twin bed on the opposite wall. Sam still lay in the middle curled under the covers. She smiled. His future was wide open now. No more fear, no more worries. All he had to do was be...Sam.

And she was going to make sure he had the chance to do that. Her phone pinged and she looked down at the screen. A long text from Kat. Nice job on stopping Pirhadi. Our techs got into the virus and it was a doozy. It was geared toward crashing the banking system nationwide and had they succeeded, it would have been an economic disaster for the United States. Tell Sam he's a hero. You both are.

Amber sank back onto the bed.

Her job was important. She did good work and she helped people. So, what was she going to do? How was she going to manage to do her job, keep her cover and take care of Sam?

"Merry Christmas! Anyone awake?" Clay called. She heard the door slam. "Hey, Mom."

She rushed from her room to the top of the stairs. "Clay?"

Her brother appeared at the bottom. He looked pale and worn and his arm was in a sling, but he was alive and had a smile on his face. She raced down to hug him. "You're all right?"

"They tell me I'll live."

"If Sabrina doesn't kill you for getting shot."

Clay's wife appeared beside him and smiled up at Amber. "I told him he gets a pass on this one, but if it happens again, he's toast."

"Are the kids with you?"

"Of course," Clay said. "Mom told them that they could make a beeline for the tree and try to guess their presents. They didn't hesitate." Jordan, Tony and Maria were the children Clay and Sabrina had adopted three years ago. Eighteen-month-old Hannah crawled over to Sabrina and pulled up on her jeans. Sabrina picked her up and kissed her cheek.

"Let me get Sam and we'll be down in a few minutes." She returned to the room and looked down at the little boy she'd agreed to raise. "Oh Lord, please help me be what he needs," she whispered. "Show me what I need to do."

Sam stirred, and Amber went to him. "Ready to go celebrate with your new family?"

He blinked up at her. "Christmas. Presents."

"Yes, I'm sure there's something under the tree for you."

"Game."

"We'll see." She uncovered him and touched his forehead. No fever. "Let's get dressed."

Thirty minutes later, she and Sam walked downstairs to find everyone at the breakfast table. Including Lance. He smiled at her and she returned the unspoken greeting.

Sam went to the vacant chair next to him. Amber took the one across from him. Amber's mother smiled a brilliant smile. "I can't believe we're all here."

Seth and Tonya had joined them with their son, Brady. Amber's veterinarian brother Aaron had arrived with his wife, Zoe, and ten-year-old Sophia. Zoe looked radiant—and about to deliver her and Aaron's new child at any moment. And her cousin, Becca, who now held Clay and Sabrina's toddler on her lap.

The family was growing by leaps and bounds.

"I can't believe you managed to fit us around this table," Clay said.

Amber agreed. It was definitely getting to be a tight fit.

Her father laughed. "I can't believe Amber is here with us for Christmas."

A hearty amen echoed through the room and Amber felt their love wash over her. They teased, but they meant well. "Hey, I was here for Thanksgiving."

Her mother let out a very unladylike snort. "Last year! You missed the last one. I hope the story was worth it."

Amber looked at Sam. "It was," she murmured. Her

parents had accepted Sam without too many questions. She'd told them about Nadia, her friend who'd died and left her custody and while they'd expressed their sorrow at the loss of her friend, they'd simply welcomed Sam into the family.

Lance caught her eye and smiled.

Clay patted her shoulder.

"Well, she's here now." Her father waved a hand at the older children. "We'll let the kids take their food into the den in just a minute. Your mother set up a table for them in there. But first, let's say grace."

Her father asked the Lord's blessing on the food and thanked Him for keeping them all safe. Amber blew out a breath. If he only knew. She added her silent thanks to the prayer. Once dinner was over and she'd helped her mother in the kitchen, Lance motioned for her to get her coat. Curious, she did then checked on Sam. He seemed happy enough to be playing chess with Jordan. She caught the teen's eye and gave him a thumbs-up. Jordan smiled and went back to the game.

Lance was waiting for her on the front porch. She stuffed her hands in her pockets and joined him. "Your parents aren't disappointed you're not there today?"

"No, my sister and her family were at my brother-in-law's folks, so they couldn't make it until tomorrow anyway. Mom and Dad are fine with delaying the celebration a day. I'll drive in tomorrow morning." He paused. "They said they were going to a Christmas church service."

"Oh, that's wonderful, Lance."

"Yes. Maybe they've been listening to me after all. When I mention God and the fact that they need Him."

"It sounds like it. I'm happy to hear that." She looked

around and her gaze landed on the barn. The temperatures were still in the fifties today and the snow continued to melt. "Hey, follow me."

"What?"

"Come on." She headed for the barn and heard him follow. Once inside, she went to the ladder and crawled into the loft. Hay drifted down but she ignored it as she spotted the area she was looking for, and bent at the waist, walked over to it.

Lance stayed behind her. When she came to the wall with the hidden area, she ran her hand over the wood until she felt the small hole. She slid a finger in and pulled. The eight-by-ten piece of wood fell onto the hay. Amber reached in, pulled out a small box and opened it. She held it up for Lance to see. "How hard was that to find?"

"Too hard for Clay it seems."

"Hmm. I'm guessing he didn't find it on purpose."

A small smile played around his mouth. "Could be."

She couldn't be mad at him. She had to admit she didn't know where she and Sam would be right now if it wasn't for her brother and Lance.

She settled her back against the wall and sighed.

"How's your head?" he asked.

She grimaced. "It still aches, but it'll pass."

"That was too close, Amber. You could have been killed."

"I know."

"So what are you going to do?"

She shook her head and looked across to the other side of the barn. "I don't really know what I'd do if I didn't work for the agency. I mean, it's not that I don't have options, but I just...don't know."

"So, you'll stay with the agency?"

"For the moment. Clay's offered to help with Sam if I decide to stay."

"I see."

She fell silent. And wondered what he was thinking. "I love you, Lance," she said softly, "I always have in a schoolgirl-crush kind of way, but our recent little adventure has just shown me the kind of man you really are and that love has managed to grow in spite of the danger and the craziness." He didn't say anything so she clasped her hands together and watched the horses in the stalls below. She'd laid her heart out there, taken a risk and was glad she'd done it.

But she couldn't deny the swarm of butterflies she now had trapped in her stomach. She pressed a hand against her middle and blew out a low breath.

Why wasn't he saying anything?

Lance knew he was probably an idiot for not jumping on Amber's words, taking her in his arms and kissing her silly. He wanted to, but the memories of his wife's betrayal were deep. And Amber planned to walk out of his life and back into a job that could get her killed.

But...

He lifted a hand and cupped her chin. "Thanks for sharing your heart, Amber."

She locked her gaze on his and nodded. "You don't have to tell me you love me—"

"But I do."

The words slipped from his lips. And once they were out, he realized how true they really were. All of a sudden the hesitation was gone and relief filled him. He smiled. "I really do." Krissy's betrayal was but a distant memory. Amber's pure heart and unconditional love had swept it away.

Joy exploded in her eyes then faded. "But?"

"But nothing. You're just going to have to help me. We're going to have to figure out how to make this work." She nodded and he swiped a stray tear from her cheek. "We can do this, can't we?"

"I think so." She sniffed. "I want to."

"I want to, too." He leaned down to kiss her then pulled back. "Do you and Sam want to go to my parents' house tomorrow to celebrate Christmas with them?"

Amber's brilliant smile nearly blinded him. "We'd love to."

EPILOGUE

6 months later

Lance spotted Amber standing ankle-deep in the water of the man-made lake just beyond the steps of the cottage. She was renting the place from her parents while she figured out what she wanted to do with her life.

She'd returned to the agency and completed one mission with them before turning in her resignation and returning home to Wrangler's Corner. She'd said it just wasn't for her anymore. And Lance had to admit he was glad. At this point, he knew he would have supported her no matter what she'd decided to do, but was relieved she wasn't going to be putting her life on the line on a daily basis.

He grimaced. He knew that was a double standard. Being a deputy wasn't exactly guaranteeing he'd walk in the door at night, but still…he wouldn't deny he was happy with her decision. And Sam seemed to be flourishing, as well.

Sam, slathered from head to toe in sunscreen, played on the sandy beach area with Becca, Amber's cousin whose purchase of the Updike ranch had finally gone through three months ago.

Amber pushed her sunglasses up on the bridge of her nose and turned. When she spotted him, her smile lit her face and she waved. "Lance!" Her reaction warmed his heart as surely as the sun heated his skin.

Sam looked up as Lance approached and a smile flickered at the corners of his lips. "Lance. Play chess today, okay?"

Lance flung his towel to the sand and ruffled the boy's hair. "Sure thing, little man. Hi, Becca."

"Hi, Lance." Her auburn curls had turned to fire in the sun and he thought she might have a few more freckles across the bridge of her nose. "How's the horse business?" he asked.

She shrugged. "It's fine." But a shadow crossed her face and Lance wondered at it. Then she shot him a smile and stood. "Speaking of horses, I've got to get back to it. I have a class starting in an hour." She gave Sam a hug and Lance was happy to see the boy let her.

Becca said her goodbyes to Amber and Lance turned his attention to Sam once more. "Hey, kiddo, what's one hundred fifty-seven times sixty-three?"

Sam looked back at the sand. "Easy. Nine thousand eight hundred ninety-one."

Lance shook his head.

"Do you really think you're going to find a problem he can't solve?" Amber asked.

Lance laughed. "No, not anymore. It just never ceases to amaze me that he can do that. It's fun to watch him do his thing."

She smiled at Sam. "He's pretty amazing, isn't he?"

"*Amazing* is a good word for him."

"What brings you by?" she asked.

He reached out and hooked a gentle hand around her neck and brought her in for a kiss. He'd never get enough of her. Her taste, her smile, her quirky sense of humor that he'd discovered she had once all the stress had been lifted from her. And her loyalty, her sense of doing the right thing no matter what. Taking responsibility for Sam was no small thing, but she'd promised her friend and she'd keep that promise to the best of her ability.

Once he'd realized that he felt the way he did, his decision to come see her today had been fraught with excitement and a nervous anticipation. He pulled back and smiled into her eyes.

"Lance?" she asked. "What's going on? You look funny."

He laughed. "Let's just say, I realized something."

"What's that?"

"That I like having you and Sam in my life."

She sucked in a breath. "Well, good. We like having you in ours." She paused. "It took you this long?"

He chuckled. "Of course not. It just took me this long to come to my senses. Which is why I wanted to ask you something."

"Okay." She blinked up at him. "What?"

"Will you marry me?"

"Yes," Sam said while Amber gasped, her heart pounding in her chest. All the air seemed to have been sucked from the atmosphere. She looked down to see Sam standing next to her and Lance. "Yes," he said again. "Say yes, Number One Mom. Say yes... Mom." He stared at the sand even as his words floated upward.

Amber gasped then laughed. She thought she might

cry. Sam had been much more verbal over the last several weeks. She wasn't sure why, but thought it might have to do with the fact that he felt secure now that the adults around him were much less stressed. And he loved the horses on her family's ranch where they'd been living for the past six months. He'd also made a couple of friends at the church they'd started attending. He would always be autistic, but he was growing and learning and it thrilled her to see it.

She raised her eyes to look at Lance. "I've loved you for what seems like forever, you know. And now you've gone and made me speechless. Why ask me now?"

"Because I'm sure. I don't want to live without you or Sam in my life. I can see the contentment in your eyes and the fact that leaving the CIA isn't something you regret."

"No, I don't, but I didn't think you'd ever marry again. Not after Krissy."

He sighed. "I didn't think I would either. Then God dropped you and Sam into my universe and rocked it off-kilter."

She knew her face was flushed from the sun, but she felt the heat from his words add more pink to her cheeks. "And that's a good thing, right?"

He kissed her again and Amber wanted to simply melt into him. She could kiss him all day. But he had other plans. "It's a very good thing," he murmured against her lips. "I love you, Amber. And I love Sam." He pulled back. "So? Do you need time to think about it?"

The sudden anxiety in his eyes and around his lips grabbed her. "No, I don't need time to think about it." She smiled at the sight of Sam back at his sand creation, working on expressing what only he could see in his very special mind. "Sam and I would be thrilled and honored to marry you. We love you, too."

He grabbed her in a bear hug and the air whooshed from her lungs. "You scared me there for a minute."

"I did not," she mumbled against his chest. "You knew I'd say yes."

His laughter rumbled against her ear then he was looking down at her again. Amber felt a small arm go around her waist. Sam had come back and had one arm around her and one around Lance. Tears choked her then fell freely from her eyes. Hope was a wonderful thing. Happiness and hope. Gifts from God. Lance was blinking rapidly and she sniffled a laugh.

Lance picked Sam up in his strong arms and Sam went rigid then relaxed. "Chess now?" he asked.

Lance nodded. "Chess now." Sam looked at Amber with a quick glance then back at the sand. "Wedding soon?"

She laughed again. "Yes. That sounds like a great plan."

"I know," Sam said. "I'm amazing."

Yes, yes he was.

And so was God. Amber decided her life was complete.

* * * * *

*If you enjoyed CLASSIFIED CHRISTMAS MISSION,
look for the other books in the*
WRANGLER'S CORNER *series by Lynette Eason:*

*THE LAWMAN RETURNS
RODEO RESCUER
PROTECTING HER DAUGHTER*

Dear Reader:

I hope you enjoyed reading Lance and Amber's story as much as I enjoyed writing it! I loved writing Lance a healing story. He'd been through so much pain with the betrayal and eventual death of his first wife that I knew it would take someone super special to make him give up on the idea that he should be alone the rest of his life. And I knew that someone special was Amber. Of course she had her own baggage to deal with, but who doesn't? We all have our issues, but it's how we handle them that determines what the future will hold for us. Lance was still somewhat bitter about his past and yet coming to an acceptance of it as well when the story began. He had found some contentment when Amber dropped into his world and rocked it to the foundation. But Lance stood strong and his true character came out and he behaved like the hero he was meant to be, not based on his own power, but because he relied on God to be his strength. I pray that if you find yourself in a tough situation where you are faced with choosing bitterness or letting God heal you, I pray you choose God.

And thank you for choosing to read this story. I pray God's blessings over you.

Lynette Eason

*When an ordinary trip into the Montana mountains
leads to a deadly game of cat and mouse, can
wilderness expert Zane Scofield protect himself and
Heather Jacobs...or will his dangerous past doom them
both?*

Read on for a sneak preview of
BIG SKY SHOWDOWN
by **Sharon Dunn**, *available January 2017 from
Love Inspired Suspense!*

Zane Scofield stared through his high-powered binoculars,
scanning the hills and mountains all around him. For the
last day or so, he'd had the strange sense that they were
being watched. Who had been stalking them and why?

He saw movement through his binoculars and focused
in. Several ATVs were headed down the mountain toward
the campsite where he'd left Heather alone. He zeroed in
and saw the handmade flag. He knew that flag. His mind
was sucked back in time seven years ago to when he had
lived in these mountains as a scared seventeen-year-old.
If this was who he thought it was, Heather was in danger.

He could hear the ATVs drawing closer, but not coming
directly into the camp. They were headed a little deeper
into the forest. He ran toward the mechanical sound,
pushing past the rising fear.

He called for Heather only once. He stopped to listen.

He heard her call back—faint and far away, repeating his name. He ran in the direction of the sound with his rifle still slung over his shoulder. When he came to the clearing, he saw a boy not yet in his teens throwing rocks into a hole and screaming, "Shut up. Be quiet."

Zane held his rifle up toward the boy. He could never shoot a child, but maybe the threat would be enough.

The kid grew wide-eyed and snarled at him. "More men are coming. So there." Then the boy darted into the forest, yelling behind him, "You won't get away."

Zane ran over to the hole. Heather gazed up at him, relief spreading across her face.

Voices now drifted through the trees, men on foot headed this way.

Zane grabbed an evergreen bough and stuck it in the hole for Heather to grip. She climbed agilely and quickly. He grabbed her hand and pulled her the rest of the way out. "We have to get out of here."

There was no time to explain the full situation to her. His worst nightmare coming true, his past reaching out to pull him into a deep dark hole. The past he thought he'd escaped.

If Willis was back in the high country, he needed to get Heather to safety and fast. He knew what Willis was capable of. Their lives depended on getting out of the high country.

Don't miss
BIG SKY SHOWDOWN
by Sharon Dunn, available wherever
Love Inspired® Suspense books and ebooks are sold.

www.LoveInspired.com

LISEXP1216